PRIDE

AND

PERILOUS

A KYLE CALLAHAN MYSTERY

By Mark McNease

DEDICATION

For Margaret McNease
whose passion could be
as frightening as it was inspiring.

1920-1999

For the readers, be sure to visit Kyle's world at:
www.KCallahanMysteries.com

TABLE OF CONTENTS

Chapter One

BLUEJACKET, OKLAHOMA - 1978

The summer had been particularly hot, even for Oklahoma. Corn had withered and died on the stalk, acres of land had choked and killed many crops, leaving others so feeble the farmers who subsisted on them had been forced to charity. Predictions were made from pulpits across the state that if ever there were clear signs of the End Times, this fever baking the landscape was surely among them.

The four Stipling children could only pray for cooling rain and fan themselves with paper fans their mother brought home from the Baptist church they attended. Clement Stipling, their father, considered the use of electricity to power fans an extravagance and a waste of money. Air conditioning was for rich people, and the Stiplings would never be rich. Clement had even refused to donate to the church's special collection two years ago for a new ceiling fan. Paper on sticks worked just fine for him, and it would work for his family.

The Stiplings were poor but proud. Clement worked as a handy-man sometimes, other times as a farm hand, and every now and then as a carpenter, bringing in enough to pay rent on their small house and put food on the table most days. His tall, wiry frame, his natural agility and his unusually large hands made him well suited for physical labor. He'd never learned a trade, nor studied anything at the knee of his no-account father. He had left home at fourteen and never looked back, which made for thirty years of staring straight ahead, taking whatever next step there was to take. Those steps had gotten him a wife, Pearl, and four children, ages two to thirteen. He was about to be a father for the fifth time, if Pearl made it through, which was looking less likely with each passing minute.

Pearl Stipling was an obedient woman. That was probably the most descriptive thing to say about her, and the virtue, as she saw it, of which she would be most proud, were pride not a sin. Humility, perseverance, and obedience. If Pearl knew what a mantra was, those three words would be it. She had humbly submitted to her life as Clement Stipling's wife, even though she was pretty enough to have found several alternatives – or so she'd been told. Middling height, with a kind face and just enough plump to her to attract men looking to raise children, Pearl had been a prize in her youth, and marrying Clement had been seen by her parents as a waste of that prize. Running off with him to elope in Tulsa was the only significant act of disobedience in her entire life, and one she had been forgiven for once the grandchildren began to arrive.

She had persevered for thirty-two years of her own difficult journey. She had been obedient, foremost to the Lord, and secondly to her husband. She loved her little ones, even though Jeffey was officially a teenager now and would not kiss her anymore except on the cheek. Doreen was ten, Emiline eight, Jessica two, and now, God willing, they would finally have another son, whom they had decided to name Kieran, after Pearl's late grandfather. Pearl, in her innermost thoughts she shared with no one and hoped God could not hear, wanted no more children after this. If Clement insisted, of course she would bear them, and if God saw fit to keep her pregnant, she would obediently stay that way, but she sure hoped the fifth time was the charm and that a second son would be the end of her child-bearing.

The way the delivery was going, it might well be the end of Pearl. She had gone into labor three weeks early. It had caught them both off guard and unprepared to get her to the hospital. Clement Stipling did not own a car, which he considered even more of an extravagance than an electric fan. He walked everywhere he needed to be, and if that place was too far he hitched a ride. There was always someone willing to take him; they knew Clement Stipling wouldn't distract them with useless talk, since he was a man of few words and the ones he spoke were seldom entertaining. So it was that on an extremely hot Thursday morning while Pearl was making breakfast, her water broke and she plunged into the hardest, most painful, most prayer-inducing labor she had ever experienced. None of the others had been like this, and two hours into it, as she lay in their bed sweating through the sheets, she knew something was wrong. She knew this would certainly be her last, as there would be nothing left of her when it was finished.

Clement Stipling had not delivered any of his children. He had done repair work and house painting to pay off Doctor Simonson for bringing his other four into the world, but to be in his own bedroom, in his own home, desperate to have this child come out already and stop this terrible experience, was something from a dream worse than any he'd ever had. He sent Jeffey off to the neighbors to call the hospital (since telephones were a waste of time and money), only to be told the doctor was in surgery. Pearl was bedridden by then, and it was just her and Clement, trying to free her body from the baby who wanted to rip her apart and at the same time stay safely inside her.

Mrs. Jansen, the neighbor woman, arrived a half hour into it. She was helping Pearl, or trying to, while Clement paced back and forth by the closed door. It was bad enough that his children could hear Pearl's screams, he didn't want them seeing any of this. Back and forth, back and forth, while Mrs. Jansen just kept telling Pearl to push. Something was terribly wrong. Well, yes, Clement thought, that's pretty obvious. Terribly wrong.

And just about the time Kieran was willing to let go and exit his mother, Pearl saw the sky open up, in the ceiling! It was the strangest thing she'd ever seen, but not frightening at all. Like a very bright skylight, like a window in the plaster, and it slid open, and there was Jesus. Smiling at her and waving. She knew then her belief had not been in vain, her faith not wasted. She knew, too, there would be no more children, no more hardship, and no more Clement.

"What is she looking at?" Clement said, standing at the foot of the bed as Mrs. Jansen midwifed Kieran Stipling into the world. She ignored him, too busy with the birth. "What are you looking at?" he said to Pearl. She ignored him, too, immersed in the joy of her own liberation as she reached up as far as she could, took the hand of Jesus, to whom she had been most obedient all her life, and walked away into the clouds.

The baby did not cry, even when Mrs. Jansen slapped him to get him breathing.

"She's dead," Clement said, staring at the frozen rapture on his wife's face. His voice was cold, flat and fierce. Within those two words were accusation, statement, and promise: he promised then and there never to love this child, never to give it warmth, never to forgive it. Not *him*; it. It was a thing, a murderous thing that had taken from Clement Stipling the only treasure his trying life had ever known.

Clement was not the drinking sort, or he would have slipped into a bottomless bottle then and there. Instead he slipped into himself. By day's end he was a widower, alone with five children, one of whom he would just as soon be rid of. The child had taken Pearl from him, and he never felt the slightest obligation to repay the theft with love. He didn't love little Kieran and never would.

That was how Kieran Stipling grew up, knowing he had killed his mother and that no prison term would ever be as harsh as the sentence his father handed down. He was hated by the man, ignored, berated and belittled. Clement never raised a hand to him, but the looks were cold enough to freeze the deepest recesses of space, the words sharp enough to bleed a man out on the spot. Kieran would never amount to anything, his father told him. He was no good, bad blood, and a gott-damned cripple to boot! The sooner he was grown and gone, the better. At the age of fifteen, Kieran granted his father's only wish for him and left home; like his father, he never glanced back.

Time passed, the road hardened, his father's prediction – his curse? – came true as nothing became of his son, his *it*, losing job after job, hustling to survive with the assistance (for it could not be called kindness) of strange men. And now, twenty years later, at the age of thirty-five, the boy who would be no one, stained at birth and declared a failure from his first breath, was about to make his mark.

Chapter Two

A Rainy Night in Brooklyn

It had been five years at least since Devin had worried about being followed. That's how long he had been living as Devin 24/7. Denise Ellerton had ceased to exist – officially, legally, physically, psychologically, and every other way in which each person functions in the world. For Devin, she had ceased existing long before that, when he had realized as a teenager that he was not like other girls; that the simple reality of pronouns was different for him, as he thought of himself as "he" while everyone else insisted on calling him "she." Tom-boyish Denise, odd Denise, rough-and-tumble Denise. He had wanted to correct them then, and even younger, as early as the third grade. "I'm not a girl," he had wanted to say, but it wasn't until he was in college that he fully understood what was going on with him, and when he finally had the distance from his family to do something about it.

The sensation of being shadowed down a dark street was one of those things that belonged to Denise, to women. Devin had long been aware of the differences in experiences men had from women; to suggest there were no differences was to choose denial over reality. There were experiences unique to men, and experiences unique to women, as well as experiences unique to those who did not fit readily into either. Devin had become a man in every way possible. The transition had been made, the journey completed, and not since before it had he worried about being followed down his own Brooklyn street, late on a rainy Friday night. There was something different about this, too. It wasn't random, as if he'd crossed paths with the wrong person in an accident of fate, as so many people did who found themselves the victims of crimes of opportunity. Devin had the very distinct and unsettling feeling that the man coming up slowly behind him had been there for awhile, had followed him off the R train, along the platform, up the stairs, and now, six blocks later, nearly to his apartment on Prospect Avenue.

Devin was tall at five-eight, and worked out religiously at the local New York Athletic Club. He'd had a trainer for two years and always believed he could handle himself in a tight situation. Not that it happened often: he didn't drink, didn't stay out late unless he had a showing of his artwork or was attending one of a friend's exhibits; he hadn't dated in three years, and he was a night person, meaning he worked at night in his studio apartment and made every effort to be home by 7:00 pm, when he would start his routine of coffee-fueled creativity, putting together his latest collage or designing a multi-medium piece that he would then spend the next two or three weeks bringing to life.

He was an attractive man, too, or so he'd been told enough times to believe. His natural height was complimented by a thin frame, short black hair he gelled back, a high, wide, forehead, moist brown eyes that had never been bothered by glasses, a thin but ready smile, and a nose that had once been broken in a fall, although he told everyone it had been a boxing match. It was the one lie he allowed himself. He just liked the idea of having a nose broken by a fist in a boxing glove. And it made the person who had once been Denise all but unrecognizable.

He'd stayed out later then usual tonight and had been cursing his lapse in discipline when he first realized someone was behind him. This stretch of Prospect Avenue, unlike nearly all streets in neighboring Manhattan, was sparsely populated at night and the presence of other people was noticeable, especially other people who were shadowing you. He'd become aware of the man behind him not long after coming up the subway stairs but had thought nothing of it at the time. Then, a block later, he could hear the footsteps, as if he were in some B-movie thriller and a stalker was shortening the distance between then. Now, four blocks from the subway and just one from his apartment building, he became convinced he was the object of the man's attention. Had it not been so worrying it would have been interesting: why would a strange man be following a reclusive artist down a deserted Brooklyn street on a rainy Friday night? He decided to ask the question directly. He adjusted his umbrella, with its caved-in side to his back, letting rain trickle down and soak his jacket, and he turned around to get a look at the man he now knew was his pursuer.

As Devin turned to face him, the stranger stopped. He was only about thirty feet away now. Devin saw that he did not have an umbrella, but his face was hidden by a hoodie pulled down over it. In late April the air was still chilly at night and most people wore jackets, sweaters, other clothes that kept them warm in the cool darkness. Hoodies were especially popular, but also had the disconcerting effect of hiding the person's face. It was only human nature to want to know who was beneath the hood, and why he was covering his face.

The man made no attempt to pretend he was not following Devin. He didn't keep walking with a turn this way or that; he didn't cross the street and continue; he didn't even keep coming, as someone would who really was just walking along the same street at the same time. He stopped. In the rain.

"Who are you?" Devin shouted, tilting his umbrella back to show himself and improve his line of sight.

The man just stood and, Devin assumed, stared. It was dark out and raining, and neither could see the other with any great clarity.

Then the man began to walk toward him.

Decision time. Devin could run for his apartment, which was only a block away; he could call for help, someone would throw open a window and call 911 – or would they? – or he could do what he decided to do and stand his ground. He was tough, he trained two hours, three days a week; he was quick and fit and thin, and above all he was not Denise, not anymore. He had not endured the challenges of his life, the demands of simply being and becoming who he was, to flee in front of some punk on a Brooklyn street. He eased his shoulders back, loosened his grip on the umbrella to free his hands, and prepared for a fight.

The closer the man got, the more familiar he looked. He was wearing jeans, red sneakers and the green hoodie, and although his face was hidden, something about his overall presence rang a bell. There was also the limp, if that was the right word, a way of walking that made it appear one leg was shorter than the other, but housed more in the pelvis, a sort of up and down motion, like a piston misfiring every time the man took a step. Devin noticed the emblem on his sweatshirt, a rainbow flag with wording underneath it he couldn't read. He relaxed; it must be a neighbor after all, or someone coming to visit a neighbor. At the very least the stranger was gay and, by inference, non-threatening.

But still he had not responded to Devin's asking him who he was. And he had stopped, then kept coming. He was only about ten feet away now, and Devin put it all together: the walk, the sweatshirt, and finally, as the man drew close and eased his hood back – the face.

"You!" Devin said, startled.

"Yes, me," the man replied, now face-to-face in the rain.

"Why are you following me?" Devin said, still trying to piece this puzzle together in his mind. He knew the man, but not really, not in any but a passing way.

"I'm following you, Devin," the man replied, "because I heard the whispers."

"The whispers? What whispers?"

The man said nothing as he stepped forward and quickly slipped his hand out from the sweatshirt's front pouch.

Devin had no time to wonder what the glint of metal was, where it belonged in this picture, this rainy night in Brooklyn, before the knife blade entered between his ribs. Once, twice, a final total of sixteen times as the man he knew but didn't know reached his free hand around Devin and pulled him close, stabbing and stabbing.

Anyone watching would think two men were hugging each other goodbye, a familiar sight just about anywhere in New York City. But no one was watching. No one saw the man ease Devin, now unconscious and quickly bleeding to death, down to the sidewalk and carefully drape him there, then turn as easily as he'd come and walk away.

"So much for art," the man mumbled to himself, clutching the knife in his shirt pouch. He turned and began heading slowly back the way he'd come. He would not take the train, but instead walk, walk all night if he had to, over the Brooklyn Bridge and back into the darkness of Manhattan, pulling the night ever more tightly around himself as he thought about the next one.

Chapter Three

WEDDING BELL BLUES

Kyle had been fretting about the wedding for two months, ever since the sudden decision had been made for the two of them to marry. It wasn't unexpected; they'd been talking about it for the past year, but now that it was upon them he hoped they'd made the right decision, that it would be, as every cultural assumption about wedded bliss predicted, the happiest day of their lives – a day to remember, not a day to regret.

He and Danny had rented tuxedos since neither of them could fit into the ones they owned. Kyle had never worn one until he met Danny, but once they began going on cruises together it was a must-have for the formal dinners: at least once on every cruise the diners would dress to the nines, giving the evening the odd feel of a doomed celebration (Kyle always imagined the ship jerking suddenly as it hit an iceberg, the diners pretending not to notice and carrying on with their fancy meal).

"I'm feeling especially confined in this," Kyle said, as Danny adjusted his bowtie. Danny was a good six inches shorter than Kyle, who was not a particularly tall man, and he had to lean up on the toes of his spit-shined shoes to get a direct look.

"Well you can't blame weight gain," Danny replied. "We just rented these yesterday." He stepped back and nodded with satisfaction at the tie adjustment.

"In a hurry, at that," Kyle said. "If I'd gotten it last week like I meant to, I'd know it was too tight. Jesus."

"Just relax. It's nerves, Kyle, that's what has you feeling trapped, not the penguin suit."

Danny stepped back and examined his partner. Not bad. Kyle Callahan was still as handsome as ever to Danny, though both would admit it was a plain-handsome. Kyle still had a full head of hair, and, like most men his age, he wore glasses. He had a slightly high forehead, and he wore his hair brushed back with just a touch of pomade, opening up a soft, inviting, and distinctly intelligent face. Standing in front of his "perpetual fiancé" as he now called Danny, he suddenly had a flash at what they might look like at their own wedding when it came.

"I know this is hard for you," Danny said quietly.

"It's not hard. I'm very happy for David. Elliot's a great guy, and being the best man ..."

"At the wedding of your first love, yes, I'm sure you have no mixed feelings."

Kyle had moved to New York City from Chicago nearly thirty-three years ago with his then-boyfriend David Grogan. David wanted to be a journalist and insisted he must go to Columbia – all serious journalism students went there, or to another of a select few schools that turned out the true stars of the profession. And while he never became a journalist, let alone a star, the young, ambitious David packed his things and drove the 800 miles to upper Manhattan, with Kyle Callahan following behind in his used Gremlin. Both their cars were soon sold, given the complete lack of a need for automobiles in the city, and upper Manhattan was immediately traded for Brooklyn, where rents were halved from anything livable on the island. The two love birds managed to nest for just three months before David announced that he was too young for this kind of commitment; and while Kyle knew it meant there were too many other men David wanted to sleep with, he took it in stride, as devoted first-loves sometimes do. He moved out, letting David live his life as he needed to, make the mistakes he had to make, and suffer the losses. There were some devastating losses over those thirty years, too. David's partner Tom, who died from AIDS-related lymphoma in 1992. David's mother Patricia, who passed away on David's fiftieth birthday. Jobs, moves, over a decade of being single for both of them, and now ... Kyle the best man in David's wedding. Life was nothing if not surprising, when you just gave it time.

They both turned toward the door when they heard Joshua start singing "Bridge Over Troubled Water" by Simon and Garfunkel. Joshua was Elliot's twenty-two year old son, soon to be David's stepson. From what David had told him, Joshua and his sister Clarice, eighteen and heading for UCLA in the fall, had accepted their father's gayness with more of a yawn than a shock and he, David, was quite excited at the prospect of becoming a stepfather at fifty-four, especially since having children wasn't something he'd ever allowed himself to imagine. Babies were a must-have accessory with same-sex couples these days, but men like David, Elliot, Kyle and Danny were from a generation just across the border, when having kids was still an anomaly in the gay community. Now, it seemed, they were everywhere, and David was delighted to come into stepfather-hood when the kids were all grown up.

"He has a lovely voice," Danny said, feeling some nerves himself. He knew David well enough, but he hadn't been in a wedding party since his sister Jennifer married her husband Henry twenty years ago.

"Is this not weird?" Kyle said, glad they were alone in the choir room. The other men of honor, friends of David's and Elliot's Kyle did not know, had already gone into the sanctuary at Manhattan's Blessed Redeemer Church and he and Danny were the last of the wedding party still straggling behind. Maybe Danny was right. Maybe he was sad about David getting married, and he was dragging his wingtips to the last minute, postponing the inevitable.

"Is what not weird?" Danny said, aware they needed to join the others.

"The whole thing. It's so ... normal. We used to be outlaws."

Danny smiled. "I doubt you were ever an outlaw, Kyle Callahan. But you can be my Butch Cassidy any time."

"And you my Sundance Kid," Kyle said, leaning down and kissing Danny gently just before leading him out to join the happiest day of the happy couple's lives.

Kyle Callahan and Danny Durban had been together for six years this coming November. They'd met by accident at the Katherine Pride Gallery on Little 12ᵗʰ Street in Manhattan's Meatpacking District. The show that time was photography; Kyle had gone to support the photographer, a friend of his, and Danny had gone to keep things oiled with Katherine Pride, the gallery owner and a new customer at Margaret's Passion, the Gramercy Park restaurant where Danny was the day manager. Margaret had turned eighty last October and used to make these homages herself. It was good business, good relations, and good publicity: a satisfied customer was a returning customer, and one who told others.

Danny had come around a corner with a glass of white wine in his hand and walked right into Kyle, spilling both their drinks. After an initial glare, their eyes softened, their smiles spread, and four months later they were living together in Danny's apartment at 25ᵗʰ Street and Lexington Avenue, kept company by their cats, Smelly and Leonard.

Kyle was the assistant to Imogene Landis, a down-on-her-luck television reporter who would never admit to being anywhere but at the top of her game, while Danny managed Margaret's, still a hot ticket after thirty years in business. Margaret Bowman lived in an apartment above the restaurant and had all but adopted Danny as her only child, having been widowed for fifteen years with no children of her own. Danny had been with her for ten of those years and, next to his mother, held no woman in more esteem. He had taken lately to fretting over her health – eighty struck him as a mile marker toward the end of the road. There was nothing he could do about the passing of time, and he shook off his worries as he searched for Kyle at the wedding reception. The guests had moved from the church to a trendy new hotel named Heaven that had opened in Hell's Kitchen. Danny wondered if the name was some kind of wordplay, given the neighborhood, and he worked his way through the crowd in the hotel's ballroom.

Kyle saw Danny looking for him and waved him over. He was standing at one of two bars the ballroom boasted, sipping on a vodka and cranberry, marveling how the crowd had managed to balloon since coming over from the church. He was thinking it might be wedding crashers, or hotel guests who felt entitled to a party when they saw one. Behind the bartender, mounted on the wall, was a flat-screen television with the sound muted. Kyle was using the straw in his drink to play with the ice when an item on the news caught his eye. A photograph of an artist he knew had been pinned to the corner while the reporter talked into his microphone.

"Excuse me," Kyle said to the bartender, a pleasant enough man who made his living as much on his looks as on his skills (or maybe not, Kyle thought, depending on what those skills were). His nametag identified him as Todd. He looked like most of the guests in a tuxedo, but he was clearly uncomfortable in it; this was a man who belonged in faded blue jeans and a vest with no shirt.

"Yes, Sir?" Todd said, sliding a drink across the bar to a guest and moving over toward Kyle.

"Could you turn the volume up on that? Just a little. I know the person they're talking about."

Todd shrugged, sure, and turned the volume up enough to be heard without disturbing the revelry.

"Hey," Danny said, walking up to Kyle at the bar. "There you are, I was looking all over for you."

"Shhh," Kyle said, putting his finger to his lips. "I want to hear this." He leaned across the bar as much as he could, trying to get every word from the television reporter.

" ... Devin — no last name — lived just three buildings from where he was attacked," the reporter said. "The victim was stabbed multiple times. Police say robbery does not appear to be a motive and so far no witnesses have come forward."

Kyle recognized the reporter as having started on NYNow and moved on to a network. It happened with quite of few of the local reporters, cutting their teeth on the popular local station and then heading to one of the Big Three affiliates. The segment was live, and Carlos Espinoza, the reporter, had been doing these updates all morning.

"What's this about?" Danny asked.

"I know this guy who was killed. Devin. From the Katherine Pride Gallery, multimedium, transman."

"A multi-medium transman?" Danny said, surprised.

"Shhh!"

"Much of what evidence there might have been was washed away in the last night's heavy rains," Carlos said, as the camera panned from him to the empty sidewalk and up the street, showing apartment buildings, brownstones and yellow crime tape stretching across the sidewalk. "If you have any information at all on this brutal murder, please contact your local police precinct. All calls are kept strictly confidential."

Kyle turned to Danny, his brow furrowed as he thought about the news he'd just heard. "They're two separate things," he said. "Devin was a transgender man, and a multi-medium artist. That's how I knew him. Through the gallery."

"Oh, I'm sorry," Danny said.

"I didn't really know him," Kyle said. "Not in more than a very conversational way. He had a show at the gallery in January, part of the New Year New Visions exhibit Kate does every year."

"The one she wanted your photography in."

"Yes, well ..." Kyle had been encouraged by Kate Pride to finally show his photos, but he'd thought it was too soon. He was also discovering he had an ego, and being part of the New Visions exhibit meant sharing the spotlight. So he had passed, and instead was preparing to have his own show a week from now. His first show. The one, depending on the public's reaction, that would determine if there would ever be a second.

"I should call Kate."

"We're at a wedding reception!" Danny said. "Celebrating the marriage of your oldest, dearest friend aside from me. This is a happy time, let's keep it light."

"He was stabbed to death!" Kyle said. "That's not exactly light. And there's something there ... something I'm not recalling just now, but a connection."

"The only connection for us to be concerned with today is making sure David and Elliot have the time of their lives. Hopefully this wedding will be the last for both of them."

Kyle nodded, Danny was right. What happened to Devin was terrible, but he was dead; there was nothing Kyle could do about it at the moment. The police were on it. Someone would most certainly come forward with information, or an eyewitness account. Whatever connection was nagging at the back of Kyle's mind could wait. It was just about time for a toast to the happy couple.

Chapter Four

HOTEL EXETER, HELL'S KITCHEN

As Kyle and Danny toasted the blessed event of their friend's marriage, Kieran Stipling balanced on the edge of his bed in a sleazy hotel room and toasted himself from a half-pint of bourbon. He'd had to spend more of his dwindling cash to buy it, but what the hell, he thought, watching with an irrepressible smile as some hack reporter standing not ten feet from where Kieran had been last night told the city there were no suspects in the brutal murder in Brooklyn. Of course there weren't. Kieran had developed an ability to remain invisible when it suited him. He had been invisible in Buenos Aires, invisible on an uptown Manhattan subway platform, and completely invisible on that Brooklyn street where the reporter kept repeating himself every half hour. He took another swig from the bottle and wiped his chin with the back of his hand. Staying in a dump like this was no hardship; it was part of the plan, part of the way he remained unseen.

In the sanitized oasis of wealth New York City had become under successive mayors determined to fumigate it, to rid it of crime and, as many believed, a soul, there were still pockets of degeneration, islands of poverty and decay that had not been whitewashed. Among those throwbacks to a time few people missed was the Hotel Exeter, located in the aptly named Hell's Kitchen neighborhood. The Exeter was a fleabag hotel, a flophouse, where rooms could be rented for $45 a day – a sum that for many who found themselves there might as well be a million dollars.

Hell's Kitchen had become fashionable again in the 1990s, as the city found itself scrubbed clean and the hookers, drug addicts and street-level criminals pushed ever further uptown. For awhile the neighborhood called itself Clinton, but once the yuppies and the Gen-Xers felt safe on the surrounding streets they decided it was cooler to be Hell's Kitchen again. They enjoyed the thrill of living in a place with one of the meanest reputations in the history of New York City, but now without the mean. Mean can't afford the rents here, and the survival of the Hotel Exeter was a fluke of zoning and location. Sitting on a corner of 36th Street, the hotel overlooked the Lincoln Tunnel entrance and exit, which would not be exchanged any time soon for the smiling faces of Mickey Mouse and Snow White. So for the time being the hotel stood, as grimy as it had been forty years ago, a beacon to the likes of the man who congratulated himself from the edge of a bed and who had been staying there for the past three weeks. Soon he would have no money left, and that was okay with him; he only had a few more things to do, a couple of loose ends to secure. All he would need then was enough for a bus ticket far away, to some border town where he could practice his Spanish and disappear into the woodwork. For a man with the power of invisibility, it would be especially easy. His dreams, dark and bloody as they were, will have come true, and things like hotel rooms and paying for them would no longer matter.

Kieran smiled as he stared down at the cars coming off the highway, driving into the heart of the city, merging and mingling with traffic from the Lincoln Tunnel. He had long believed the people in New York were all in a mad rush to nowhere. He had lived here for five years, having arrived an innocent in many ways, believing in the power to reinvent his life. He was proof that dreams were still shattered here, and that no amount of prettifying and industrial cosmetic surgery would ever rid the Big Apple of its rotten core. That is where he had found himself, the dark heart of a city putrefied beneath the shine and glitter, and where he was now. Living in a hotel room barely large enough to turn around in, sharing it with hundreds of roaches that did not have to come up with $45 a day to stay there. The three dresser drawers were empty, except for his two changes of clothes, minus his favorite sweatshirt he'd had to throw away because of the blood. Sixteen times were simply too many to stab someone without making a mess. The room's television had never been converted to hi-def; just as well, since the cable was out and the best he could do were the local channels barely grasped by a rusted antenna. But it was enough to watch the news, enough to make him smile as he finished off his bourbon, wondering if he should spend ten dollars to buy more. He would be making a trip soon, a side journey of utmost importance and ultimate delight. He muted the TV and reached for his wallet. He deserved to celebrate a little more, and by the time he got back from the liquor store they would be running the news clip again. Murder in Brooklyn, no suspects, no witnesses. Reality television at its best.

Chapter Five

THE KATHERINE PRIDE GALLERY

Much like Hell's Kitchen, the Meatpacking District had a very Old City sound to it while having little Old City about it except a few stray cobblestone streets. The area was originally the home of Fort Gansevoort, also known as the "Great White Fort" for its many coats of whitewash. The name was Dutch, appropriate given the original settlers of the island, whose presence could still be felt in place names around the boroughs. Following the Civil War, the area became home to butchers and meat packers serving the thriving, crowded city, and these slaughter-houses gave it the name its current residents still used, even though the only meat to be found there now was on high-priced dinner plates at high-end restaurants.

Another feature of the new Meatpacking District was its shops and galleries. Nothing said Old World quite like a Stella McCartney dress shop next to an art gallery whose least expensive item was for sale at $75,000. In some ways it was an odd location choice for Katherine Pride, since she valued new artists, up-and-comers, artists whose work might go for the average week's salary of a local secretary. She showcased more established artists and photographers from time to time, but her real pleasure was in introducing someone new to the art world, and, more importantly, to the public. And if an artist went on to fame and fortune and happened to remember the break Katherine gave them, well, great, she could sell their work and make ends meet on the East Village condo she shared with her husband Stuart.

Katherine Pride had been Katherine O'Connor before her marriage twenty years ago to Stuart Pride. She'd planned to keep her own name if she married, but the chance at having such a unique and bold last name was too good to pass up. Even then, when she was working behind the ticket booth at the Metropolitan Museum of Art, she knew a branding opportunity when she saw one. She'd had no specific idea of what her place in the art world would be, but could see the name Katherine Pride emblazoned on a business even then, at twenty-three. All these years later she was still married to the doting Stuart Pride, a successful real estate broker, and the Katherine Pride Gallery was an established, well-respected gallery among her peers and in the neighborhood.

Katherine was what people often called statuesque, standing just over six feet in heels, thin and possessed of a strong posture. Her late mother had instilled in a young Kate (as most people called her) the sense that posture was destiny: anyone who wanted to go places in this world needed to see where they were going, and you don't do that by hanging your head or slouching. Stand up straight! Stand up tall! Head back! Kate and her brother Justin had heard these commands many times, and when their father died in a freak boating accident, the calls to be straight and tall only grew more frequent and more insistent. Pamela O'Connor became a widow and a single mother on the same day, when Kate was only twelve and Justin nine, and she brooked no nonsense in a world that afforded her none. That was in Louisville, where her mother managed to survive and raise two successful children, until she, too, lost her life. Breast cancer made Kate and Justin O'Connor orphans much too young.

Kate quickly made her way to New York City after college. She didn't know then what she wanted to do, but she knew exactly where she wanted to live. New York City was the epicenter of art, fashion, literature and finance. Somewhere in there was her future, and not long after she began working at the Met she knew which one it would be: art, for art's sake and for profit, for better and for worse in a fickle world that loved you one minute and pawned you the next. She was a gallery owner who kept her distance from the sharks and the scene, a wife who loved spending evenings with her goofy, lanky, adoring husband more than attending another cocktail party for another shining star. Still, she loved the gallery and what it could offer people like Kyle Callahan, the photographer she'd befriended after meeting his partner, Danny Durban. Kate and Stuart had enjoyed lunch at Margaret's Passion some years ago, their first time there, and who should show up at a gallery exhibit two days later but Danny Durban. She knew it was marketing, making sure a customer came back, but she had liked Danny straight off, and she took great pleasure in having been the catalyst for his relationship with Kyle. They had met at that exhibit and were still madly in love. Or at least in love enough to be sharing their lives together forever and ever, Amen.

Kate had been encouraging Kyle to show his photographs to the public. He was a bit shy, but with a definite gift for images. She would never have known this if Danny hadn't told her, and even once she had seen Kyle's pictures it had taken a few years of nudging to finally get him to accept that he should have his own show, which was now only four days away.

Kyle was waiting with two cups of coffee when she got to the gallery at 10:00 a.m. Monday morning. One thing about businesses in New York City: they may stay open until midnight, but finding much besides diners and drugstores open before mid-morning was a challenge. Even the Katherine Pride Gallery didn't open until 11:00, but Kate had wanted to go over the details and exhibit photos with Kyle before the final installation.

"You're alone today," Kate said, fishing a key ring from her oversized black purse. Danny usually came with Kyle on these visits and would head from there to Margaret's Passion.

"Danny's on vet duty. Smelly has some kind of nasal infection," Kyle said, referring to one of their two cats. Smelly had been with Kyle when they met, and Danny had been spending his life alone with Leonard,

Smelly's senior by three years. Smelly was a she, and Kyle had found her as a kitten outside his apartment in Brooklyn, digging through trash that had seeped onto her coat, giving her the name. He'd thought about changing it to something else, Gloria, or Smittens, but Smelly had stuck and he never gave it a second thought now.

"She's sneezing a lot. And he's getting her weight checked again."

"She's diabetic, yes?"

"Pre," Kyle replied. "But she's been pre-diabetic since she was two years old. She's just an ample girl, I think."

Kate slid open the iron gate that protected the front glass, unlocked the door and led them into the gallery. "I see you brought me coffee from Breadwinner's. Very thoughtful."

"I'm used to getting Imogene's on the way to work," Kyle said, following her into the reception area and setting the coffee cups down on the front desk.

"How is she, by the way?" Kate asked. "She moved up or something, you said, after those murders in New Jersey."

"Pennsylvania. Pride Lodge. Yes, they were quite the hit in Japan. She's on the general news beat now."

Kyle had been the personal assistant to Imogene Landis for the past five years. A diminutive woman whose height was overshadowed by her personality, she was once a successful TV reporter in New York, but had a habit of telling her bosses and anyone else what she thought of them, their competence, and at least once, their toupee. She subsequently found herself on the downslope of a career that could have kept rising, had she been more politically savvy. Now she worked as an English language reporter for Tokyo Pulse, a cable TV show that aired in Japan three hours before sunup and was produced by Japan TV3, who had their New York studio on 46th Street. Kyle met her there most days with two cups of coffee from their local spot, Cecil's. Kyle had tipped Imogene to the murders at Pride Lodge last Halloween. The story caused a cult sensation in post-midnight Japan and got her off the financial beat. She was back into the city she loved, covering everything from City Council meetings to bathtub decapitations. She couldn't be happier.

"You're good to her, Kyle, I hope she appreciates it. Danny, too."

"Oh, I'm sure they do. I didn't even have to coerce Danny into the vet visit this morning, and that's something he always wiggles out of. He hates doctors' offices, even when they're for the cats."

The Katherine Pride Gallery looked like most galleries. It's all about wall space and lighting. A dividing wall here, some pedestals there, and you have your basic art gallery.

Kate had gone into business on her own eight years ago. Before that she was an assistant to the late, great Hildegarde "Hildy" Bingham, the woman who had single-handedly discovered most of the top geniuses of the New York art world in the 1970s. She was already old and well past legend status when she hired Kate as her personal assistant. Kate had studied at the feet of an art world icon, spending many evenings on the floor in Hildy's Upper West Side penthouse, taking notes for the autobiography that was still unpublished nearly a decade after her death.

"When's Corky come in?" Kyle asked, referring to the young man who worked the front desk at the gallery. Corky was somewhere in his mid-twenties and loved – absolutely loooooooved – working at an art gallery, for Katherine Pride, in the Meatpacking District, a neighborhood he only knew in its sanitized state. Corky very much wanted to get married, but he didn't have a boyfriend and had reminded Kyle more than once that he was on the market, should Kyle or Danny know anyone with a suitable income.

"I gave him the day off," she said, setting her large brown leather purse on the front desk chair. "He had a wisdom tooth removed Friday and he's still mending. Funny thing to call it, the boy doesn't have a lick of sense in his head."

"Wisdom comes with age. Sometimes not even then."

"So," Kate announced, waving her left hand toward the walls as she flipped the track lighting switch with her right.

Kyle turned and marveled at his own photographs on the walls. He'd seen them when they entered, of course, but having them lit now, a penlight aimed at each individual photograph, sent an unexpected charge through him. He saw himself as a shutterbug, just a guy with a camera who liked taking pictures. A couple years ago he took the next step and started putting them on a Tumblr photoblog, AsKyleSeesIt, with no intention of ever presenting them in any professional sense, and none of charging money for what he loved to do.

Frowning suddenly, Kyle said, "What if they hate them?"

"Who's 'they', Kyle? You mean the critics?"

"Never having displayed my pictures before means never having read a review of them. So yes, the critics."

"You know as well as anyone we do these things for love. Your photographs, Stuart being a real estate agent in a city stuffed with them, me running an art gallery. It's all because we love doing it, and sometimes we make some money. What other people think of what we do really doesn't matter." She sipped her coffee. "And if the guy from the New York Times calls you an amateur, well ... you are!"

Kyle looked at her, horrified, just as she winked to let him know she was joking.

"Now let's take a slow tour through the rooms and see what all the fuss is about with this Kyle-Somebody."

They started with the first photograph, left wall as people would enter the gallery. It was among his favorites, but also an emotional reminder. "Lonely Blue Pool" was the picture he had taken of the empty swimming pool at Pride Lodge, the pool where his friend Teddy Pembroke had been found dead just last Halloween, his neck broken from a shove into the cold, waterless pool.

"I still can't believe it's not a painting," Kate said, staring at the photograph. It was what everyone said when whey saw it: an expanse of blue, with just a white ladder running down it and a gathering of brown leaves at the bottom, near the drain. So simple, and so beautiful.

Kate and Kyle were watched from across the street as they made their way further into the gallery along the wall. Kieran thought he would feel excited to be this close to his prey, this close to winning a game only he knew he was playing. Devin knew, of course, but Devin was dead. He'd recognized Kieran just as the knife was coming out, and the puzzled look on his face was immediately replaced by fear and terror.

What whispers?

The ones I heard when you thought I wasn't listening.

What whispers?

The ones that sealed your fate.

"You want a refill on that?"

He jumped, startled by the young barista at Breadwinner's who had stopped by his table while he stared across the street, lost in his thoughts. They didn't have waiters at coffee shops like this, but she was wiping down the tables and happened to notice his empty cup. He turned and saw how pretty she was, her long curly hair held back with a purple ribbon, her brown eyes liquid and trusting. If he'd been into women he would put her at the top of his list, but he wasn't, and the only list he was keeping was getting shorter and shorter as he killed the people on it.

"No, thank you" he said. "But I appreciate your asking. It's a rare courtesy these days. Nobody gives a shit anymore. You give a shit, it's very touching."

She wasn't sure how to take this man and there was something disturbing about him, not least the way he was speaking to a stranger who had only thought to ask him if he wanted more coffee. She smiled nervously and headed back behind the safety of the cash register.

He turned back to the window and saw that Kate Pride and the Callahan guy were gone, having turned at a dividing walling into the next room. He would get to her soon and hoped it wasn't a situation where Callahan was with her when the time came. He didn't want to kill an innocent man – as far as anyone can really be innocent in this life – but he would if he had to.

Kyle was happy with the layout. He and Kate had chosen the photographs carefully over the last two weeks. He'd been sure to include one of Danny's favorites and one of his mother's favorites. The other thirteen, for a total of fifteen of his best pictures, were lined along the walls in a way that reflected not so much a progression of any style, but a small set of subjects. Two from his shoe series, in which he took shots of people's shoes as he went about his daily life in New York City. Three from his "blur period" as he called it, when he was fascinated by blurred photographs, a few of his seasonal photos, and the best of his interiors – rooms, hotel lobbies, office buildings, and two cathedrals. It was a fair and solid representation of Kyle

Callahan, Amateur Photographer, and as much as Kate wanted to believe she'd found another rising star, Kyle wasn't invested in the outcome. He just loved taking pictures.

"I have to head to the studio," he said, letting out a deep sigh.

"I thought you loved your job," said Kate, misreading the sound.

"Oh, the sigh, no, that was for the show. The people. The nakedness of it all. My mother's coming from Chicago, Danny's parents from Queens, our friend Detective Linda from New Hope, it's too much."

"You'll be fine. And trust me, you'll want more. The limelight can be intoxicating. Just don't become addicted."

Kyle hugged his friend and mentor, for Kate Pride had become both, with her encouragement and her insistence that Kyle take himself seriously as an artist. He was thinking how lucky he was to have Danny, his mother, Kate, so many supportive people in his life, when he noticed a man across the street in front of Breadwinner's, staring at them. "Who's that?"

But as quickly as Kate released the hug and turned to the window, the man was gone. "Who's who?" she said.

"Nobody, really. Just someone I thought I recognized." He tried to think of where he would have seen the man, but nothing clicked and he let it go. "Speaking of recognizing someone, it's terrible about Devin, I saw it on the news."

Kate's smile fell. "Yes," she said. "Horrible. No one would want to hurt Devin intentionally, he was a sweetheart. All that rough and tumble, it was just attitude. The guy was a creampuff. It had to be the wrong place at the wrong time."

"I'm not so sure," Kyle said.

"Why's that?"

"Something keeps nagging at me, another death, but I can't remember it. We'll talk about it later, maybe you can help me jog it loose. I have to be at the office ten minutes ago. Imogene's one virtue is punctuality."

They hugged a last time, and Kyle wondered, as he breathed in Kate's subtle perfume, if anyone was ever truly in the wrong place at the wrong time.

Chapter Six

MARGARET'S PASSION

Margaret's Passion had been at 21st Street and 3rd Avenue in the Gramercy Park neighborhood for thirty years. The park itself was only a block away, occupying a private, gated rectangle that was one of the most historic and famous in a city filled with landmarks. The area was once a swamp, and a developer named Samuel Ruggles proposed the idea to drain it and turn it into a park. "Gramercy Square," as it was first called, is now held in common as one of the city's two privately owned parks, which the general public must enjoy by gazing at it through wrought iron bars.

Margaret's restaurant had been a number of businesses over the hundred years the building had stood. Some of its previous incarnations included a pub, a bookstore, and a haberdashery. Margaret and her husband, Gerard, first leased the space, while living in one of the twelve apartments on the three floors above it – theirs being directly over the main dining area and accessible by a staircase they had built in the rear of the kitchen. After ten years of success, the Bowmans bought the building, which became a curse as well as a blessing. Neither of them had any experience as landlords and they finally hired an agent to manage that unwanted part of the business, which left only the restaurant for Margaret to deal with after Gerard died.

The death of Gerard Bowman was a greater blow to Margaret than she had anticipated. The man she had spent nearly fifty years of her life with, first meeting him when they were both still teenagers, had been a lifelong smoker. She was able to get him to stop smoking in their apartment, which led in a way to his untimely death. It was while smoking on the side of the building that he was run over by an impatient livery driver. It had been raining, and he had walked to the curb to stamp out his cigarette butt. Just as he was doing that, a black sedan came flying through the light, determined not to have to wait for the next one. The driver lost control somehow and plowed into Gerard. He died instantly from a head trauma, the one mercy the Bowmans were given from that terrible day.

Margaret wasn't the same after her husband's death. Already short and thin, she all but stopped eating, and reached a critical point when her doctor threatened to have her hospitalized. Her hair, naturally graying, became all white, and while she kept it long and tied back with ribbons most of the time, it began to fall out. She was determined to keep Margaret's Passion open and thriving, but it was something she now forced herself to do. A year after Gerard's death, Margaret was at a crucial juncture. She was just about to walk way from it all, including New York City, when a man come into her restaurant for lunch. His name was Danny Durban, and Margaret happened to be down in the restaurant that day. He was very cheerful, and the two of them struck up a conversation. He invited her to join him, and she did – something she had refrained from as a business policy all these years. It was one thing to sit for a moment with a dining couple or a family (never alone with a man), but eating with them in your own establishment was simply not done.

She didn't tell Danny Durban much that day. It was not her style to pour her heart out to anyone but the man who had died outside their restaurant. But he was kind, and inviting, and amusing, and experienced in the very same business. Danny was then working as the day manager at a restaurant on the Upper East Side that was struggling to survive and likely would not. As it turned out, Margaret was looking for a day manager herself: Pierre, the one she'd had for twenty-five years, had retired six months earlier and the new man, Salvatore, was not working out. She had decided to let him go but needed someone to bring in as his replacement. Meeting Danny Durban was a long-needed moment of serendipity.

Two weeks later Danny was working for Margaret, and a relationship that would shape both of their lives was born.

It was less than a ten minute walk from Danny and Kyle's apartment to Margaret's and the weather couldn't be better. While Danny enjoyed California and points west, he couldn't imagine living without the distinct change of seasons that people east of the Mississippi enjoyed. The East Coast was particularly nice. It didn't have the kinds of harsh winters you found in Chicago or Minneapolis, yet there was never any question which season you were in; and of the four, only summer made Danny wish he were somewhere else. The heat and smell of summers in Manhattan could be nasty.

Margaret's Passion had the feel of a restaurant that had been running successfully for three decades. That comfortable, settled feeling was part of its attraction. Like a number of other well-known eateries in Manhattan, it valued its place in the neighborhood, as if it were an old friend who, along with the residents, had weathered good times and bad and managed to survive. There was a large bay window looking out onto 21ˢᵗ Street, through which passersby could see people dining, conversing, and eating some of the best food in the city. The entry was narrow, reminiscent of its pub days, and just inside was the lectern where the maître d' greeted guests. It was dark wood, matching the rest of the wood in the restaurant's interior, and – so Margaret claimed – had belonged to the church in Poughkeepsie where her parents' married hastily just before her father went off to combat in World War I.

Chloe was on duty today when Danny got there late after taking Smelly home from the vet. She was the senior day waitress and a real pro, making each diner feel as if they were the center of her attention, and for it pocketing tips that kept her living in style.

Danny waved good morning to Trebor, the bartender, who was behind the long oak bar serving a few early customers. Trebor was the youngest of the people working in the restaurant, aside from some of the kitchen staff, and had been with Margaret's for four years now. Danny had poached him from one of Linus Hern's restaurants. Linus was Danny's nemesis, and the restaurateurs' version of a vulture capitalist: he got restaurants off the ground, then sold them for a profit and quickly vanished, leaving nearly all of the buyers bankrupt a year later with "Closed for Renovations" signs in their windows, which meant they were never coming back. Danny knew the future did not look good for Trebor and offered him a job, telling him as discreetly as possible that the restaurant he was working in, having been sold by Hern, was in all probability doomed. It was only after Trebor started at Margaret's Passion that Danny discovered it was Robert spelled backward. Clever boy.

Chloe made a cup of coffee for Danny, a routine she had that he had not discouraged, and set it on the table closest to the kitchen. That was where the two of them would usually have coffee and go over details for the day. The menu didn't change, but there was a checklist Danny adhered to faithfully. It was also their time for some casual conversation before the lunch crowd showed up.

Chloe took a seat, stirring cream into her coffee. "He was back this morning," she said. "Her new lawyer. And he wasn't alone."

Margaret's longtime lawyer, a man named Evan Evans who had been with her since she and Gerard opened the restaurant, had passed away nine months ago at the age of eighty-six. The old gentleman, whom Danny had always found to be as mischievous as he was gracious, had been a weekly figure there for many years. He would come in for lunch every Thursday, eat alone, then head upstairs to visit with Margaret. He was as much a companion for a woman whose companions had nearly all died as he was an attorney. At that age the wise tend to make preparations, and he had suggested Margaret hire a young lawyer named Claude Petrie – the man who, Chloe had just explained, had come in again to see Margaret, this time with two other men.

Claude bothered Danny, though he couldn't say why. He was not much taller than Danny, but considerably heavier. He could always be found in a suit and tie, with a briefcase in his hand, although Danny had the feeling it was for effect and probably empty. Claude seemed to need people to think he was very busy, and of late that might be true: he had been to see Margaret several times the last month, never for very long. Unlike the man who had recommended him, Claude did not dally, did not sit for a leisurely lunch on the house, and spoke little to anyone, including Danny.

"Something's up," Danny said to Chloe. She nodded, having concluded the same thing.

"Estate stuff?" she said. Margaret was now an octogenarian and likely sensing her own mortality these days.

"I'll find a way to ask her," Danny said, a dark mood starting to descend. He couldn't imagine life without Margaret, and the thought of it reminded him his own parents were getting old. Once they were gone, he and Kyle were next in line. That's the way it went in the human carnival.

Fortunately customers began to arrive, pushing thoughts of funerals and grieving periods out of his mind as he rose to greet them with a smile. Ever pleasant, ever present. Just another lunch Margaret's Passion.

Chapter Seven

HOTEL EXETER, HELL'S KITCHEN

The reporters had moved onto another story by Monday afternoon. New York City had been cleaned up over the last twenty years, but it was still the nation's largest city, with plenty of crime stories to shock its jaded citizens. Kieran didn't care; he had watched the same reports of the murder he had committed enough times to be bored by them. Brutally stabbed, sixteen times, no leads, call this hotline, blah blah blah. He was just waiting for them to say a reward had been posted, contingent on his capture and conviction, and they could check off all their little murder story boxes and move on.

Kieran wasn't interested in watching television, anyway. He was interested in the man in Philadelphia who had answered his ManCatch ad. He had used one of the computers at the internet café on 9th Avenue, which was really just another overpriced, pretentious coffee shop with mouse turds in the muffins and a couple bolted-down laptops customers could use for .50 cents a minute if they didn't bring their own.

ManCatch.com was a symptom of a society gone digitally wrong, where no one really had to meet anyone unless there was an exchange to their mutual benefit, usually of bodily fluids, and where everyone could pretend to be someone else. That's what he'd done, placing an ad on the Philly page of the website, posing as exactly the kind of young man Richard Morninglight would notice immediately: barely legal, with an aw-shucks tone in his message they both knew was a put-on. Roles, games, players. For thirty or so words he had played the part of a young college student trying to pay the bills, for which he would gladly be an escort, no harm in that, and if anything untoward happened, well, he was a willing student of experience. He knew this is what Morninglight enjoyed, and sure enough, not long after the artist arrived in Philadelphia for a show that would take his career several steps up the ladder, he responded to Kieran in New York, not knowing where he was. Among the Internet's dubious advantages was that you could be anyone, and anywhere. *Hi, Kevin*, Morninglight wrote. *I'm at the Hamilton Inn the next few nights for a convention* (of course he wouldn't tell the truth) *and would love to help out with the cost of those college books! Email me back and let's see what we can do.*

What they could do, it turned out, was arrange for Kieran, posing as Kevin the college student, to arrive at Richard Morninglight's hotel that night. As soon as Morninglight knew he was downstairs, he would leave his door unlocked, slip naked into his bed as if he were sleeping, and wait with every cell of his body tingling in anticipation.

He probably won't even open his eyes, Kieran thought as he gathered his Latex gloves, the guitar strings he'd bought that morning, and a change of clothes in case things got messy. Morninglight will think the man climbing into bed on top of him is there at his pleasure, just another pretend college student making ends meet. But no, Richard, he thought. The pleasure will all be mine.

He zipped up the gym bag, grabbed his brand new hoodie from the bed, the one with "I Love NY" stenciled on it that he picked up next to the liquor store, took one last look around a room he would soon be checking out of forever, and headed to the bus terminal for the ride to Philly.

Chapter Eight

APARTMENT 5G

"Stop staring at me," Danny said. "You should know after all these years the sad-eyes routine won't work with me. And judging from the size of you, neither does this diet cat food."

He was standing at the kitchen sink having just given Smelly, their rotund six-year-old tiger, her evening ration of dietetic cat food that was costing them $2 a can from the vet. Smelly no longer smelled badly but she was eighteen pounds heavier and nothing they had tried seemed to slim her down. Danny often described her as a bowling ball with legs, a barb she ignored. She sat staring up at him, her pleading eyes calculated to get at least a small cup of the dry food her feline housemate Leonard enjoyed, fed separately behind a closed door in the bathroom. Leonard indulged his status as the alpha cat and could often be seen throwing a smug glance back at Smelly as he was put in the bathroom with a tasty dish of calorie-rich dry food for only him to savor.

"I really don't have time for this," Danny said, as Smelly did her usual approach-and-retreat to her food bowl before hunger finally made the decision for her. She caved, walked over to the food bowl and began eating. She would only tolerate this treatment for so long before she would find a way out of this place, this prison of veterinary design, and live freely once again among the trash bags. They may think it an idle threat, as she had many times dashed into the hallway when the front door opened, only to panic at the great unknown and come slinking back in. But she meant it, damnit, and if they insisted on feeding her this awful, tasteless mud, she would make it to the stairwell next time, through the door, down the stairs and out, and who would be sorry then?

"What are you doing in there?" Danny shouted. Kyle had been in their second bedroom, one they used as an office except for the rare occasions when company came. One of those occasions was upon them; Kyle's mother, Sally Callahan, was arriving Friday from Chicago to be at the opening of his photo exhibit and they still needed to get the room in order. Absent a guest, it tended to get sloppy, dusty, and generally used.

"A photograph, what else would I be looking for in here?"

"A book maybe," Danny said, wiping his hands on a dishtowel and heading into the room. "Papers of some kind."

They had turned the second bedroom into an office shortly after Kyle moved in. He had been the one to give up most of his furniture and belongings, since there was simply not enough room for two full apartments in one, but he had insisted on a working space of his own. He needed a room with a door he could close while he spent hours working on his photographs, cataloging his photographs, archiving his photographs. He was rarely without a camera around his neck or in his backpack, and had long been in the habit of shooting hundreds of pictures to get a few good ones. Images were like that: so many flashed by in the course a day that you had to grab as many as you could and hope for a diamond or two. Even the same image might need to be shot ten times, from ten different angles, to find its essence.

His share of the room consisted of a file cabinet and his father's large maple desk. It was the only thing of his father's he requested; he wanted it for its history, the stains in the wood, the burns from when his father smoked, and not at all for the fact his father died with his face pressed against the desktop. An aneurism had felled Bert Callahan in a matter of seconds and Sally had come home to find him slumped over his papers, cold and departed. She was glad Kyle had wanted anything at all by which to remember his father, given the chill of their relationship from the time Kyle was a boy, and she was happy to be rid of another reminder of her loss.

The back wall that divided their respective office spaces, Kyle's to the left, Danny's to the right, with a window between them, was taken up with bookshelves. Both men were bibliophiles, Kyle more so, and it was probably his books more than anything that gave him a sense of continuity. Some of the books he'd had as a child, and he could let his eyes wander slowly up and down the shelves remembering periods of his life by reading the book spines.

Kyle was at his computer scanning photographs. He would pick one out of a dozen, enlarge it and peer at the people in it. He had learned early that the eye doesn't always know what it is seeing. In this case he was looking at people who had come to the opening night of the New Year New Visions show. He could name some of them: Devin, Richard Morninglight, Kate and Stuart Pride, others among the crowd he knew from the gallery. He was hoping to recognize the man from across the street that morning, without being sure why he thought this is where he'd seen him.

"What are you looking for?" Danny asked, resting his hand on Kyle's shoulder.

"Not 'what,' but 'whom'," Kyle replied. "A man I saw outside Breadwinner's this morning, staring at the gallery. He looked so familiar, but it was one of those things, you see somebody and you swear you know them ..."

"Happens to me all the time. Hundreds of people come into the restaurant in a week, I remember a fraction of their names."

"Not his name, so much, just where I saw him. The New Visions show, it's stuck in my mind for some reason but I don't see him in any of the photos."

"The invisible man," Danny said, as he moved away from Kyle, looking around the room. "We should get someone in to clean." He slid his finger along a bookshelf and examined the dust that came off it.

"I can clean."

"Before Friday? Your mother's coming."

Kyle sighed. Yes, his mother was coming. She stayed in this room on the sofa bed and it needed to be dusted at least. The reminder of his mother's impending arrival got him thinking of it again.

"I'm worried," Kyle said, swiveling around in his chair.

"It's not cancer," Danny said. He knew where this was going. Sally had told her son she had something to talk about. Kyle, being prone to imagine the worst, assumed she was going to tell him she was seriously ill. He was already imagining a leave of absence from Tokyo Pulse, flying to Chicago to spend a month with his ailing mother. Danny was looking forward to Sally coming out with whatever it was and putting and end to the morbid speculation.

"I never said it was cancer," Kyle replied. "But something. She doesn't keep secrets from me. Even less so since my father died."

Kyle spoke to his mother at least twice a week and always on Saturday. He had worried about her after Bert died just shy of their forty-seventh wedding anniversary. To his surprise, she had adapted well and quickly, but she was still a seventy-five year old woman living alone in Chicago and he considered it his duty as her only child to fret over her.

"She's probably moving to Florida, or San Miguel. Lots of ex-pats down there in Mexico, you can live very well, very cheaply."

"How do you know these things?"

"I listen to my customers, talking is what they're there for. Talk, food, and sometimes a chat with Margaret. Speaking of which, I think your mother is not the only one with a secret."

"Really?"

"Yes," Danny said. "Something's going on with Margaret. She's had that new lawyer of hers –"

"The rodent."

Danny smiled. He had referred to Claude Petrie as a rodent when he first told Kyle about him. "That's the one. He's been to see her several times, and today Chloe told me he was in with two other men."

"Smells like investment."

"Possibly. But in what? Chloe thinks it's her estate, that she's getting things in order. Why the two men, though? Claude could easily do a will, which I'm sure she had done a long time ago with old man Evans"

"You have to just wait and ask her."

"Exactly," Danny said. "Same with your mother. You have to wait and ask her what this big secret is. Life is change, Kyle, that's the nature of it. It's not by design."

Kyle froze suddenly, struck by Danny's words. "Exactly!" he shouted.

"Is there an echo in here?"

"No, no," Kyle said, excited. He got up and crossed to a bookshelf. "I remember now the other death, the one I couldn't think of when we were watching the news."

He skimmed along the bottom shelf and found what he was looking for. It was the catalog for that year's New Year New Visions show at the gallery. Devin was one of the artists, but it wasn't Devin he was looking for. He opened the front cover and read the credits.

"There," he said, holding the catalog up so Danny could see as he pointed to a name: Shiree Leone.

"Who's that?"

"She was the graphic designer for the catalog. Designer. *Design,* you just said it. I couldn't remember her name, or what the connection was. It was just a fly buzzing around in my head after we saw the news on Devin."

"What about her?" Danny asked.

"She's dead!"

Great, Danny thought. Here we go again. The murders at Pride Lodge were a fading memory, but a memory still new enough, and he feared Kyle would go off on another chase at precisely the worst time, with his mother coming and his show opening on Friday.

"Murdered, I suppose," Danny said.

"No. Yes. They don't know. That's what I remember. She fell in front of a subway train."

"Coincidences happen, Kyle, no matter what people say."

"But nobody saw it! There was no one else on the platform, I remember that. They were asking for any witnesses, just like Devin's murder the other night. They assumed she fell or had a seizure or something."

"But you know better."

"She could have been pushed."

"There was no one there, you said so yourself."

"No one *saw*," Kyle said. "That's not the same thing. Maybe there was someone there. An invisible man."

"I was joking. There is no such thing as an invisible man."

"Devin might beg to differ with you. And Shiree."

"Please don't say you have to find out."

"What choice do I have? This could be connected to the Katherine Pride Gallery. There could be more already dead … and more to come. I can't just wait and see what happens, can I?"

Danny did not respond. He knew anything he said to Kyle to dissuade him would fall on deaf ears. This is what Kyle did, along with photography and being a personal assistant: he solved murders. Stopping him would be tantamount to taking a thought from his head and putting it outside, go away, thought, you're not wanted here. They were Kyle's thoughts, in Kyle's mind, and nothing Danny could do or say would chase them away. Even if Kyle said he would drop the subject, Danny knew he wouldn't.

"When does Detective Linda get here?" Danny asked, referring to Linda Sikorsky, the homicide detective from New Hope, Pennsylvania, they had befriended after the Pride Lodge murders. She had since come fully out as gay and was making a trip to the city for Kyle's show.

"Tomorrow. We're having lunch."

"Good. Tell her whatever theories you have flapping around in your brain. If you're going to go running after killers, at least have back up."

"I'm not going to get hurt," Kyle said. He stepped to Danny and put his arms around him. "Don't worry about me."

"And you don't worry about your mother, and I won't worry about Margaret, and nobody will ever worry about anyone again."

Kyle took Danny by the hand. "Come with me," he said, leading them out of the office and toward the bedroom.

"Are you asking me or telling me?"

"Just start with the top button and we'll see."

Danny smiled as they walked down the hallway. It had been two weeks since they last had sex. That seemed pretty much the norm in relationships that lasted more than a few years, and they were men in their fifties, whatever part that played. It was good to know they could still cut loose when the opportunity and the desire came upon them. For the next hour he would not be concerned with anything else, including a killer whose trail Kyle had picked up in an art gallery catalog. He knew Kyle would go where it led, and the best he could do was hope he made it back safely.

Chapter Nine

A Corner Table at Osaka

L inus Hern didn't care for sushi, but the restaurateur knew his two investors were very fond of it, and it was their money he would be using in his most recent and most anticipated venture: to buy Margaret's Passion, with neither Margaret nor her flying monkey, Danny Durban, knowing it. As far as Hern was aware, Danny didn't even know the old lady was selling, and if all went well he wouldn't find out until it was too late. By then Linus could step out from behind the curtain and tell Durban his services were no longer needed. It would be a costly vindication, but one he'd imagined for years, ever since the two men first met and knew it was disdain at first sight.

Linus had made a career of starting restaurants, and in some cases taking them over, getting them ready for their big debut, which would be covered by absolutely anyone worth being called press, launching them into the nightlife stratosphere, and getting out with his investment doubled. What happened to the restaurants after that was not his concern, and most had not lasted more than a year, by which time Linus Hern was long gone, his bank account that much fatter, convincing the next investors to ride his coattails to the New York Times Food Section. He was a venture capitalist, a man of industry. He knew how to open with a bang and close without leaving a trace. A master, if he said so himself.

He was tall, even seated at a corner table. He was wearing a blood-red velvet sport coat, something as uncommon as it was distinctive, with spotless white leather jeans. His high forehead masked a receding hairline and at the same time favored his face, highlighting sharp blue eyes that just last year had undergone Lasik surgery. At fifty-six, Linus refused to wear glasses; he didn't care how fashionable they were, or which top names were designing them. Linus Hern was determined to appear a superman, a specimen of the highest order. Glasses would be a blemish in an otherwise flawless presentation.

He motioned to the waiter for another Scotch. One was normally his limit, but his venture partners were late and he needed something to sip. Late was a mortal sin to Linus Hern, but considering the amount of money they were putting into this, he would make an exception.

Osaka was the latest in Japanese fusion, whatever the hell that was. Anytime someone added a new ingredient it became "fusion." Some Thai farmer adds carrots to the pot for the first time and it's "Thai fusion." Hern disdained such labels, knowing them as a marketing ploy and only really meaningful to lower-tier food critics and the floods of trendy young diners lining up to get a table at the latest "fusion" restaurant.

He got a table, of course, probably one that had been reserved for lesser people who would be told upon arrival that there had been a mix up, so sorry, that table is taken. "That table" being the best one in the place, nineteen stories up in Midtown, southwest corner overlooking the nighttime Manhattan skyline. The City was Linus Hern's only true love; that and making money. Men were treats, tasty bonbons he enjoyed and discarded as quickly as a caramel nugget might melt in his mouth. What was the last one's name? The one he'd taken for that regrettable weekend at Pride Lodge. Carlos, was it? What a mess that whole business turned out to be. The Lodge was still standing but Linus had no idea who ran it now, and no plans to go back. Murder had a way of making a place less attractive.

He looked over and saw his partners arrive, a full fifteen minutes past due. Had they not already given him a hefty retainer with much more on the way he would have left them greeting an empty table. But he was shrewd, a winner, and rather than even glance at his watch to tell them they were late, he smiled, stood, and offered a warm hand.

"Victor," he said to the taller of the two, a man near his own height whose air of stupidity was underscored by a scar running from his left eye to his chin. The result of a car crash in his twenties, but a very effective visual when someone needed to be intimidated. (Margaret Bowman had not been among them, and took pity on the man whose face had been disfigured at such a young age.)

"Linus," Victor said, shaking his hand and taking a seat in the booth to Linus's right.

The second man was downright jolly, more than balancing any discomfort people might feel in Victor's presence. Jay Tierney was a financier, a venture capitalist like Hern, only his specialty was in demolition: tearing down the old, the decrepit, and putting up the new. Tierney was robust, affable, his hair cropped short and his face round and pink. He smiled easily and often, and had mastered the art of including that smile in his eyes, something most predators simply could not do. It was impossible to tell with Jay Tierney if his smile was fake or not, only that it was meant just for you, and you might find yourself being swallowed by it if you weren't careful.

Jay Tierney and Victor Gossett had been business partners for twenty years, with dealings that stretched from Manhattan's Lower East Side to San Francisco's waterfront. They could buy a building like Margaret Bowman's with the change rattling around in their pockets. The plan being presented to the old woman was to save her restaurant and secure her final years by buying the building and everything in it. She would have enough money to live comfortably anywhere she chose, and the restaurant would pass to Danny when she died. What only the three men at Osaka knew was that it was all a lie: Margaret's Passion would be permanently closed for renovations, and the building that had stood there for over a century would be replaced by something shiny, new, and very costly to inhabit.

It helped that her old lawyer had passed on. Evan Evans had been smart and worldly, and this particular sleight of hand would never have gotten past him. But the young one, Claude Petrie, that had been a stroke of luck. He still lived in the old man's shadow and pressured himself to make his own mark, establish his own credentials. Finding new owners for Margaret's building had been the best timing of his life. He had been on the verge of disappearing and had started looking into exactly how someone does that, when Hern showed up in his office with a proposition.

Linus had come up with the plan when he first heard rumors of the old woman's troubles. There may be 20,000 restaurants in New York City, but the world of the best is a small one. When something happened at The Greenery, or Casa Pueblo, it was known by all the others in hours. When Margaret Bowman had her young new lawyer put out feelers for a buyer, Linus Hern was among the very first to hear it. He had quickly contacted his fellow predators Victor and Jay, and in amazingly short order the three of them had formulated a plan. A plan so slick, with a truth behind it so carefully guarded, that Margaret Bowman and her sidekick Danny Durban, a man Linus could not wait to fire, wouldn't know what hit them until it was too late.

Linus again waved his hand, summoning their table server.

"I'm still waiting for my Scotch," he said to the young Asian looking woman, wondering if she was some kind of fusion, too. "Not a good sign."

"In so sorry, Mr. Hern," she said, even bowing a bit to emphasize her embarrassment. "Right away. And the gentlemen? What may I bring you?"

That was better, Linus thought, as the other two placed their drink orders. He wasn't listening. He was drifting away for a moment, daydreaming of the sweetness he would feel when he'd accomplished his greatest coup. Margaret's Passion would be no more.

Chapter Ten

THE HAMILTON INN, PHILADELPHIA

The Hamilton Inn was located in the heart of Philadelphia's gay neighborhood, an area of Philly's Center City district that ran from Market Street on the north to Spruce on the south, and from 11th Street on its west edge to Juniper on the east. It was among the nation's most well known and well liked concentrations of LGBT urban life that were once called gay ghettos. But unlike many such enclaves, Philly's had not fallen on hard times; it had seen itself prosper, becoming and remaining one of the city's most vital attractions.

Two of those attractions were the Gilliam Museum of Modern Perspective, and the Hamilton Inn, a storied old hotel that had remained gay-owned and mostly gay-populated for forty years. The late Marcus Gilliam founded his museum, which was really more of a midway point between a high-end gallery and a true fine art institution, in the 1980s during the height of the AIDS crisis. His longtime lover died from complications of the disease and left Gilliam with two dozen specimens of art so modern it wasn't worth anything at the time. Gilliam had two objectives in launching his museum: to effectively erect a monument to Jonathan, his lover and partner, and to demonstrate his remarkable eye for an invest-ment. Considering how much the art was now worth, his prescience could not be disputed. He had specialized in finding new artists, much like his peer Kate Pride in Manhattan, whom he had known for several years before his own death from prostate cancer in 2009. Since then a foundation had run the Gilliam, but it had not compromised his vision. The museum still featured a mix of established artists and those well on their way. It was just such a show that brought Richard Morninglight to Philadelphia that week-end; and where else would a gay painter on the verge of art world stardom stay in Philadelphia but the Hamilton?

The Hamilton Inn had been around since the 1920s. Its premiere suite, while no longer called Presidential, had seen its share of American Presidents resting their heads on its pillows. Just five stories high, the Inn had fallen on hard times in the 1970s and was very close to being demol-ished, when an entrepreneur and friend of the very same Marcus Gilliam who opened his hybrid gallery/museum decided to recreate the Hamilton as a specialty gay hotel. Back then "gay hotel" was something one could say, before the arrival of the acronym LGBT and before there were many people now called allies. The hotel no longer advertised itself as gay, and it made every marketing effort to welcome all visitors to the fine city of Philadelphia and this amazing neighborhood. But it was still gay-owned and operated, and rare was a visit from a guest who didn't know it.

Richard Morninglight had checked into room 306 Friday night, just about the time a fellow artist named Devin was having his life stolen at the end of a knife blade. Richard's last name was not Morninglight, but once he had decided on a career as an artist, long before he was anywhere near achieving it, he concluded that his last name Smith simply would not do. Even adding a middle initial, which remained popular among artists and writers for reasons he didn't understand, would not make the name Richard Smith any more arresting. Ah, but he painted in the morning light; he studied effects of the morning light on canvas and the objects he painted; he had a vision one sunrise in the morning light, and that was that: Richard Morninglight was born.

Richard had few real friends. He'd been ambitious all his life, even as a child, and he had known instinctively that ambition was an all-consuming master. Given the choice between achieving his aims and having friends who wanted this or that part of him, let alone a lover who wanted it all, he had chosen achievement. He'd found soon enough that there seemed to be a ratio of friends to success (one increases with the other), and as for lovers, they came cheaply enough. Ads in local papers, profiles online. Why get into the mess of a relationship when all he really wanted was his needs attended to?

He wasn't an unattractive man, and at thirty-two he was still young. He'd gained too much weight since the checks began coming in for his paintings, but not one young man had complained about the extra twenty pounds. He was middling height, with a pronounced nose, what might be called Roman, and brown eyes that were just the slightest bit crossed, something he'd had to deal with as a child wearing corrective glasses. He wore his thinning black hair long and in a ponytail – it just seemed to go with his name – and he'd gotten his first tattoo to commemorate the show at the Katherine Pride Gallery just a few months ago that had launched him into semi-fame.

Success had not come easy, but adjusting to it had. Richard had imagined the finer things for years; becoming accustomed to them felt natural, as if he had always been entitled to the best life had to offer. His artwork had been selling since he was in his early twenties, but the Pride show had taken it to another level, exposed him to people like the Gilliam's curator, in town to see what was on the art horizon. While several of the artists for the show had gained attention, Richard was one of the two real breakout stars, along with Javier Velasco. Velasco was somewhere in South America these days, maybe Argentina, wowing whomever constituted the art world there, and here Richard was in Philadelphia, a nice enough town for a stepping stone. Now that he'd made it to the Gilliam, MOMA couldn't be far behind.

He sipped his red wine and slipped off his robe. He'd had several emails back and forth with Kevin, the young hustler who called himself an escort and who must be on his way right about now. He had already laid out the scenario with him. Richard would be naked, face down on the bed, pretending to be sleeping. Kevin would let himself in through the unlocked door – how careless of me! – and Richard would be startled, feigning panic just as Kevin scrambled onto the bed and held him down. So helpless. So exciting. He eased down onto the bedspread, slipped his hands under the pillows, and waited for the sound of the door opening.

Kieran never cared much for Philadelphia. History was its only real selling point. If you didn't care where the Constitution was signed or who the hell signed it, Philly was just another big city with funny accents and greasy food. He admitted to enjoying its skyline, though. He had a fondness for skylines; they represented for him a far away place he had almost arrived at, a destination of soaring towers and deep, shadowed canyons. For some it was as if they were going into a land of light, neon and fluorescence; for him it was a descent into night. He felt safest then, when no one could see him. His power of invisibility was strongest in the darkness, when onlookers strained to see and he became a shadow among shadows.

He arrived at the bus station just as the sun was setting. All bus stations seemed the same to him. On the upside, they tended to be seedy. Someone with a limp and a filthy backpack, unshaved and gaunt, was just another Joe coming off the bus. One among hundreds.

He made his way to the Hamilton Inn and stood outside looking up at its lush green awning. There was only a tasteful, polished brass plaque on the building to announce its presence in the neighborhood. Pretense, he thought, as he walked quietly and quickly along the side of the building to where he knew there was a service entrance. Once upon a time this is where the dark-skinned dishwashers and laundresses, the hotel maids and the chauffeurs, made their way to the hotel basement from where they would fan out on their duties, always around and always unseen until needed. He knew about the entrance from a reconnaissance trip two weeks ago. He knew as much about the people on his list as he needed to, which was much more than they would ever know about him. He knew where they went, when they went, and how often. He knew Richard Morninglight stayed at the Hamilton, and that he enjoyed the company of unfamiliar young men when he did. It had been easy; too easy, and he felt a certain disappointment that there wasn't more effort needed. He would have to take his satisfaction in the killing itself and leave the challenge to the last one, the one who would see him in broad daylight. Unlike the fool Morninglight or the hapless Devin, startled by recognition into thinking he'd come as a friend and not an executioner.

There would be no description from the desk clerk because he did not stop at the desk. He pulled his hood over his head and made his way through the side entrance, down the cellar stairs and up in the freight elevator. He doubted anyone at the desk even noticed the elevator was moving, if they bothered to monitor it at all.

He got off on the third floor and walked quietly to room 306. As he stood in front of the door, he slipped his backpack off and reached inside for the set of six guitar strings. He carefully took out the thinnest of them, a slim, deadly piece of silver wire, held it in his left hand and walked into the room.

Richard heard the door open. He was on the bed, naked, as arranged, with his head turned toward the wall and his eyes closed. He could feel his heart race as he pretended to sleep, anticipating the "attack" they'd agreed on. The only person he'd ever told about these get-togethers had said it was dangerous, but he assured them, no, the men came by the desk, there were video recorders everywhere, nothing was going to go wrong.

Kieran stood over Richard, cocking his head and examining the artist's body. It wasn't much to look at, he decided. He wondered if Richard tipped the young men who played this game with him. He could use some extra cash and might have to take a gratuity whether it was offered or not. He gently laid his backpack on the floor and stretched the guitar string between his hands.

Something felt off to Richard. He'd expected a giggle, a word of hesitation. He feigned waking up and raised his head, turning to see someone he vaguely recognized, and it was not a beautiful young man come to play.

"What the fuck are you doing here?"

Kieran may be lame but he was fast and lean. Before any real resistance could be mounted, he jumped on the bed and straddled Morninglight, who was trying to turn over. It all happened so fast. In seconds he was firmly on top of the artist and he'd looped the guitar string over his head. All he had to do then was pull.

"You can't talk now, can you?" he said to the frantic man trying desperately to throw him off. "No more whispers. No more looks. Who's looking now? I am!"

Richard Morninglight flailed as best he could, but his attention was divided: his body was trying to buck the man on his back, while his hands were clawing at the metal string around his neck digging deeper and deeper. Nothing more was said; it was all done in a strangely silent tableau, with only the bouncing of the bed to make any noise. Soon it was over, and Kieran hopped off Morninglight just as blood from his nearly severed head began to soak through the sheets and mattress. For a moment he thought of taking the head as a trophy, but it would create problems and complicate what should be a swift, silent exit.

He left the guitar string embedded deep into Morninglight's neck. He went through the artist's wallet and took the $263 dollars he found there. And then, just as easily as he had come for the kill, he vanished. Paying no mind to the camera on the hallway ceiling, he was beyond that now. Back down the freight elevator, out the side door, and into the cool Philadelphia night.

Chapter Eleven

A VIEW OF THE CLOISTERS

Kyle hadn't been this far uptown in years, not since he was looking around at apartments to buy just before he left his job at TriCore. It had been a whim, really; he knew he would have to take on a stifling mortgage to afford a co-op in Manhattan. He also knew he might not last much longer at the company he'd been with for six years, the last two of them miserable as he went from working for a man he cared about and who treated him well, to working for a group of mid-level managers when his boss was let go who considered him just another pool assistant. The kind of character you'd see in movies from the 1950s, women at typewriters churning out letters for a half dozen bosses who only knew them as outboxes. When Harry was let go, Kyle wanted to go with him, but the man he'd supported with the same kind of devotion he now showed Imogene Landis didn't land anywhere. A bar stool, Kyle guessed, cursing his bad luck to get old in a workforce that discarded people over fifty. Harry had been a decade older than that, and despite getting a sizable severance package and reassurances he would do just fine, Kyle doubted his boss had what it took to claw his way back in a recession. He never knew, because Harry never told him. As close as they were from 9 to 5, they did not have an off-work relationship. He knew, too, that Harry was a proud man and chose not to keep Kyle informed of his fate. Maybe things had turned out all right, but maybe they hadn't.

Kyle left the company before he could pursue buying an apartment. It was just as well; he'd called Brooklyn home since moving to New York and he was perfectly happy to stay there. Then he met Danny, and here he was – living near Gramercy Park, in a two-bedroom apartment with a partner and two cats.

This morning Kyle was riding the A train all the way to Inwood, to visit a woman he had never met who might have information for him, but who just as likely might slam the door in his face. Her wife had died recently in a most horrible way, falling from an empty subway platform beneath the wheels of an oncoming train. It had been very late at night and no one had seen what happened. Shiree Leone died as alone as anyone can, her last emotion stark terror as a monstrous train tried to stop, its wheels screeching like some demon from Hell's basement, drowning out the sound of her screams. Alone, without a single witness, dead with no one to tell her goodbye.

The intercom in front of Shiree's building didn't work, so Kyle lingered out front in the small courtyard until someone came out. The woman looked at him with mild suspicion, either pegging him as another harmless middle-aged gay man, or simply not caring enough to ask him why he didn't have a key. She was bundled up more than was needed on a cool late April morning; she clutched her oversized purse to her side, and even held the door behind her just long enough for Kyle to enter the building with a quick, "Thank you."

The building was what New Yorkers called pre-war, meaning it was constructed before World War II. These buildings were strong, and often had the kind of detail and ornamentation not found in more recent buildings. Kyle was among the many who loved buildings like this: enormous lobby, high windows, most comprised of dozens of small panes, wide marble stairs for anyone not using the small, creaky elevator, and a fire escape at every landing. He stopped between floors and looked out to see the Cloisters not far away. He stared at the strange and magnificent museum. Built with an endowment from John D. Rockefeller to house his art collection, the Cloisters were designed to resemble a medieval European abbey. Many visitors who happened upon them and didn't know what they were, assumed they had once been a monastery.

It was a breathtaking view, and Kyle forgot for a moment why he was here. He pulled himself from his thoughts and continued up the stairs to apartment 4J.

He knocked lightly and waited for an answer. When none came, he knocked again, more forcefully.

"Who is it?" he heard a woman's voice call from inside.

"My name's Kyle Callahan," he said. "I'm with the Katherine Pride Gallery."

He was telling the truth, sort of. He had a show coming up at the gallery and was friends with Kate.

"I don't believe you," the woman's voice said. "You're a reporter. I don't fall for this kind of thing. I have nothing more to say."

Kyle thought for a moment. If she assumed he was a reporter, then he wasn't the only person who'd been around asking about Shiree Leone's death.

"I'm really not a reporter," he said, his face close to the door. "I'm ... a friend of a friend of Shiree's."

The deadbolt sounded and the door opened a crack, held in place by a chain as a dark-skinned woman with short red hair and piercing brown eyes took measure of this man at her door.

"A friend of a friend," she said. "So that means you knew Shiree exceedingly well, does it?"

"Well, no. I didn't know her at all. But I care about how she died. And I am involved with the gallery. She did their last catalog."

"I know that."

"I have a show coming up there, and an artist who was part of the last one was killed over the weekend. Stabbed, in Brooklyn. I think it's not a coincidence. Shiree dying in the subway, I mean."

"I know what you mean," the woman said. "But let me point something out to you, Mr. Friend of a Friend. You want me to speak to you about something that has been a profound tragedy for me, yet you've not even asked my name."

Kyle blushed and looked down, as embarrassed as he could remember being. "Yes, you're right. I'm so sorry. Are you Olive? Olive Washburn?" He had read her name in the news reports.

"Olivette. Please don't use the diminutive. But I won't hold it against you. And I could use company for a cup of coffee. That's as much time as I'll give you."

"And that's as much time as I'll ask for," Kyle said, as Olivette Washburn slid the chain back and welcomed this curious, gay, white, intrusive man into her home.

The apartment was cavernous, with high ceilings and arched doorways. Olivette led Kyle into the living room and offered him a seat on the couch. He glanced at a hallway leading back into the apartment and guessed there was at least one bedroom there.

A large black cat sauntered up to Kyle just as Olivette said, "Excuse me," and headed into the kitchen.

"I'm Kyle," Kyle said to the animal as it sniffed his hand. Its response told him it would not be remembering his name. The cat turned away, uninterested in the intruder, and hopped up on a brown leather recliner, curled into a ball and eased its head down on its paws.

"That's Hector," Olivette called from the kitchen. "Don't pay him any mind. He won't pay you any."

Kyle was looking around at the room, curious at how sparse it was: one maple bookshelf with three shelves given to books, the other two to photographs and knick-knacks. The cat's recliner and the couch Kyle was sitting on, which felt like a sofa bed. A plaid armchair opposite the recliner, with a coffee table between them. A few framed posters that appeared to be Shiree Leon's artwork, and a cathode-ray television that looked not to have been used for several years.

Olivette came back in carrying two cups of coffee. Kyle quickly took stock of her again, taken by how lovely she was: short red hair, a flattish face, ebony skin, black hands with nearly pink palms, and eyes that knew she was being examined, knew the difference between a fool and a friend, and that Kyle was neither. She was wearing a red sweater and black jeans, with house slippers in the shape of tigers. She smiled slightly, setting Kyle's coffee on the narrow coffee table in front of him, then taking her own to the recliner. She shooed the cat away and sat down.

"I've told the police everything I know," she said. "But you're not the police. So what is it you were wondering?"

"Well," Kyle said, trying to gather his thoughts. "Do you think it was an accident?"

"They said she jumped, that's the last I read about my wife's death."

"So you were married?"

"No," she said, smiling again. "We always called ourselves married. One for the revolution, so to speak. I don't need the state to validate my relationship. Do you? Assuming you have one."

"I do, I do," Kyle said. "My partner's name is Danny. Sometimes I call him my husband ..."

"But you think it's not real until you go to City Hall and get a license. How did we make it the last few thousand years, with our fake relationships? Makes you wonder. Anyway, I'm just being contrary. What were you saying?"

"I got to thinking ..."

"After Devin's death."

Kyle looked at her, surprised.

"I read the news, too. I don't watch it. That TV's a piece of crap and I won't pay for cable. Shiree only kept it because she said it was an art installation. She was like that."

Kyle could see the sadness in her eyes, even as she smiled at the thought of her beloved, gone forever.

"I didn't think anything of it at the time, except how terrible it was," she said. "But I read the news online and it did seem kind of strange. The whole three-deaths thing."

"When two celebrities die, a third's not far behind."

"Crazy, I know, but I thought if Shiree was one, and this Devin was a second, maybe there would be a third. So I watched for it. But it's only been two days, there's still time." She chuckled at the absurdity of it, then grew serious again. "He was a nice guy, Devin. He and Shiree weren't close, but she got to know him when she did the catalog for the Pride Gallery show."

"Well, that's the connection," Kyle said. "If there is one, I really don't know at this point. But if there is, I think the killer may not be finished. You said Shiree and Devin were friends?"

"Not friends, unless you're someone who thinks a few hundred people on Facebook are your friends when only about three of them really care what happens to you. Friendship used to be meaningful. There I go again … no, they were not friends. They formed a little group, a little bond, while the show was going. Shiree was a shy girl, and it helped her to have someone to talk to at these events. She also had to work with the artists to do the catalog. It was a short-time thing. Show closed, everyone moved on."

"Not everyone, clearly. If that show is what connects them."

"Do you think you might be next? Is that what you're afraid of? I read you're having an exhibit yourself there this week."

"It's not me I'm worried about. I wasn't involved with the January show, and I don't have any connection to the Katherine Pride Gallery, aside from being friends with Kate."

She stared at him, waiting a moment for him to realize what he had just said.

"What?" he asked, then, "Oh my God. Friends with Kate. Is that his list? But she has so many friends, dozens of friends. He can't be after them all."

"If it's about Kate Pride and the gallery, that narrows things down a bit."

"It is and it's not," Kyle said, suddenly sure. "It's about *that show*."

"New Visions."

"Yes, the New Visions show. Something about that show and the people involved."

Olivette took a moment to weigh her words, caressing her coffee cup. "How well do you know Katherine Pride?" she asked.

Kyle was surprised by the question. "Not terribly well. She's a friend, and a mentor, of sorts."

"Yes, a mentor. That she is. She likes to encourage people."

"Is there something wrong with that?"

Olivette shrugged. "Not if you're the person she's encouraging."

Not if you're the person she's encouraging. It was an enigmatic statement, and one Kyle decided not to question for now. It could have several meanings and he preferred to ponder it rather than pursue it and appear hostile.

"Was there anything different the last few days of Shiree's life?" he asked. "Anything out of place that either of you noticed?"

"Like the man she said was following her?"

Kyle stared at her.

"She couldn't prove it. She couldn't even describe him. It was more a *presence* she felt, the last two, three days before ... the fall. The slip. The push. The shove. Take your pick."

"Did you tell the police?"

"Of course I told the police. But this guy was a phantom. She said he looked familiar, but she couldn't say how. He wore a hoodie, she couldn't see his face. It was the way he walked."

"The way he walked?"

"Like a rooster, she said. Cocky like, but wrong, like he was off balance."

"Was she close to other people involved with the January show?"

"Nah," Olivette said, finishing her coffee. "Shiree was a freelancer and a loner, except for me. She did a job and moved on. She got friendly with a circle at the Gallery while it lasted. Devin. This cat named Richard Morninglight, whose real name was probably Jones. These artists can be so full of shit."

"So you're not an artist?" Kyle asked.

"No, no. I'm MTA. Transit Authority. I'm a bus driver."

Kyle suddenly realized how much of our perceptions of others are built from assumptions. He would never have thought Olivette Washburn was a bus driver. He didn't like making assumptions. Deductions, yes. Intuitive guesses, certainly. But assumptions were not only unfair, but could get you killed.

"I'm going to leave you now," Kyle said, having gotten what information he could from Olivette.

"You're on the right track," she said.

"And what track is that?" Kyle asked, as he slowly stood from the couch.

"That Gallery. That show. Maybe even that woman."

Maybe even that woman. Did she have something against Kate Pride, or had Kate Pride wronged her somehow? And if she had, had she wronged a killer as well?

Olivette walked Kyle to the door. The moment she was out of the chair, Hector traded places, hopping up on her chair and curling into a ball on the warm cushion.

As Kyle was about to leave, he pulled a business card from his wallet and handed it to her.

"Japan TV3," she said, reading the card. "Personal Assistant to Imogene Landis."

Kyle cringed. He had never liked having that title on his card, but Imogene insisted.

"I dig that chick," Olivette said. "Saw her on TV at my mother's house. Did a story about some murders at a gay hotel."

"A lodge. In Pennsylvania."

"Well, I'll be. She's a piece of work, that one. You can just tell."

"Yes, you certainly can."

Olivette held the door open for him.

"If you think of anything else," Kyle said.

"I try not to, to be honest. But if I do, I'll call Imogene's assistant, don't you doubt it."

Kyle saw a gleam in her eye, a hint of mischief, and it came as a relief. Olivette Washburn would survive. He suddenly wished they'd met under different circumstances, that the coffee they shared could have been over a very different conversation.

"Thank you again," he said, as she nodded and closed the door behind him.

Chapter Twelve

PENN STATION

Detective Linda Sikorsky had not been to New York City in thirty-five years. Her last visit was with her parents, to see a production of "A Christmas Carol" and tour the light-strewn city in mid-December. It was the most magical time to be in Manhattan, with giant toy soldiers guarding street crossings and reindeer flying over Fifth Avenue. It was also three months before her father was gunned down in an act of random violence outside a grocery store in their hometown of Cincinnati. They'd flown to New York for the occasion, Linda, her father, Peter, and her mother, Estelle. It had been planned for a year, and the anticipation had built through September, October, November, until finally Linda burst off the airplane in Queens and never stopped talking about all the things she saw on the taxi ride into Manhattan. So magical had it been, and in such horrible contrast to the death of her father the following March, that Linda had never come back.

Pete Sikorsky had been a Cincinnati cop for fifteen years when he was shot outside a corner grocery, off-duty, an innocent bystander killed in a senseless act of violence. It was a nightmarish bookend to the time they'd had in New York, and Linda had never wanted to see the city again. Not when she lived in Ohio, not when her mother remarried and moved them to Philadelphia, and not when she became an officer on the New Hope, Pennsylvania, police force. A mere two hours away by car, less by train. It was as if she could look out her kitchen window and see, far in the distance, the city that had put a divider in her life between the good and the evil, the before and the after. For her New York City would always be a perfect memory followed by a perfect loss, and the fragility of it had kept her away, until she met Kyle and Danny.

All these years later she was living a life she would never have imagined that glorious Christmas thirty-five years ago, followed so soon by the defining tragedy of her father's death, and it was time to chase away the ghosts. She put her misgivings aside and took the train from Trenton to spend four days in Manhattan, to think about her new relationship, and to see Kyle and Danny, whom she had befriended during the Pride Lodge Murders – as they'd come to be known. In part because of Kyle's boss, the overbearing television reporter who managed to revive her career with a story about the killings, and in part because it was an easy thing to call them. "The Murders at Pride Lodge." She admitted it had a ring to it, and had even toyed with writing a book about it. Maybe she would do that when she left the New Hope police force, something she'd been discussing with Kirsten, and something she wanted to talk to Kyle about.

Kirsten. The other thing she wanted to talk about. The woman she met at a New Year's Eve party four months ago, and who was now Linda Sikorsky's first official girlfriend. Linda had wanted her to come along, but Kirsten wasn't quite ready to meet "the family", and both of them felt there would be plenty of time for it. Linda believed Kirsten would also be the only girlfriend she would ever have; she knew the odds were not in their favor, given the survival rate of relationships in general. But their ages – Linda at 43 and Kirsten at 47 – played into her thinking as well. They were not school girls in the throes of a crush. She had known she was lesbian pretty much all her life, but she had never acted on it. Not out of any doubt or self-loathing, but because she had lost someone she loved so completely – her father – at such a young age, that she associated love with pain. To love someone was to accept that you would eventually lose them, or they would lose you; it was as inevitable as death itself, and while Linda knew that might be a morbid way to look at it, it was her truth. Until Kirsten. Until she became aware that some pain down the line was worth the joy that could be found living in the present.

Linda was a tall woman, six feet in her stockings. She had let her blonde hair grow out since last October and wondered what Kyle would make of it. She'd become a bit more feminine, if that's the word, influenced by Kirsten's sense of style and ease with a makeup case. She was still what was her mother called a big-boned gal, but she had trimmed down a bit. Having a woman like Kirsten McLellan by her side made her want to look her best. Kirsten turned heads, with her ramrod bearing, her svelte physique, startling green eyes sprinkled with flecks of yellow, and her style. Kirsten was a real estate broker whose presence spoke high-end: she sold only the best, to only the most demanding. Kyle had even mentioned it as another connection between them all: Kate Pride's husband was a real estate broker, too. Kyle was always looking for connections, as if he saw the world in dots, or pixilated patterns that could be brought into focus by staring at them long enough. Oh look, your girlfriend sells real estate, and the husband of the gallery owner who's showing my photos sells real estate, it must mean something! To Linda it simply meant the world was smaller than most people think, and nearly all roads cross if you just stay on them long enough.

Kirsten was successful and demanding, yet her heart was as true and generous as any Linda had ever encountered. Kirsten McLellan knew how to win, that's all, and when she was alone with Linda she turned that sense of competition off. The two women had nothing to prove to one another, and everything to enjoy. It was Kirsten who encouraged Linda to consider leaving the police force. Linda had long imagined opening a store in New Hope and spending her days talking to shoppers, selling them vintage finds she'd bought at auctions and flea markets. Not antiques, God no; Linda didn't know an antique from an old piece of furniture. But she loved perusing aisles and bins, sifting through drawers and racks of gently worn clothes. She even had a name for the place: *For Pete's Sake*. Named after her father, naturally. She would add some kind of sub-title, maybe *Vintage Everything*, something to tell people when they saw the store sign exactly what they were walking into. It was her dream, her fantasy, and until Kirsten came along she'd always kept it locked away. Maybe not much longer.

Her train pulled into Penn Station just as Kyle was getting back on the subway in the northernmost reaches of Manhattan, having learned enough from Olivette Washburn to know he was onto something. They had arranged to meet for lunch at a diner called the Stopwatch, a block from the station. She was early enough to have time to check into the hotel – she had paid for early arrival – and maybe even a short nap before heading to the restaurant. She had a lot to think through and already her nerves were on edge. She had wanted Kirsten to come with her, but there would be plenty of time and opportunity for them all to meet. They could come back in the summer, or get Danny and Kyle to visit New Hope again. They could even stay at Pride Lodge. It had changed managers since the killings, but the old man Jeremy who had been the silent partner in the whole affair still owned it.

"They'll love you, Kirsten" Linda whispered to herself, hoping it to be true. How could it not be? Linda Sikorsky was level headed. Linda Sikorsky was an excellent judge of character. Love was not blind this time.

She eased up from her train seat and reached for her luggage in the overhead rack. All would be well. Kirsten was everything she'd fantasized in a partner. She was back in New York City and excited to see how it had changed, considering how little she remembered of it from her childhood. She was going to her friend Kyle's first photography exhibit. Renewal and happiness were in the wind.

Chapter Thirteen

Hotel Exeter, Hell's Kitchen

Kieran watched the people on 36th Street six floors below hurrying for the sake of hurrying, as was the case with nearly everyone in Manhattan. He had noticed when he first moved here that everyone was in a mad dash to nowhere, thinking themselves terribly important with terribly important things to do. People didn't so much walk on the streets of this city as maneuver, quickly circling around and through one another to get to the same destination five seconds faster. The first rule of life in New York was to *seem* to matter. To give the impression to anyone who might be looking, while assuming everyone was, that you had some- thing to do right this minute. You were one of the busy people. There were only three stages of being here: up-and-coming, already arrived, or dead. He had never been the first two, and hoped the third was a long way off, but he had observed it around him since the moment he first arrived as a man without a home. Oklahoma was no place to go back to, and New York City was no place to stay. Between the two he had lived – drifted, really – from Salt Lake City to Seattle to New Orleans, never staying long enough to leave much trace of himself. Wherever he ended up, he would be on the run, and that was okay with him. He had been running all his life.

He hadn't slept since returning from Philadelphia at one o'clock that morning. He'd thought he might, given how tiring it was to strangle someone. The only people who seem to know that are the people doing it. Everyone else experiences murder in the abstract, as part of a movie or a television show. But to actually straddle a man and nearly decapitate him with a guitar string, now that will exhaust you. He padded naked from the window into the bathroom for a third cup of instant coffee, made with hot tap water. He couldn't afford real coffee, the kind that tasted good and didn't make you feel like it was corroding your stomach. The kind that didn't make you puke. He had been throwing up more lately and wasn't sure if it was from the wretched instant coffee or from the excitement of killing people he'd been planning to for the past two months.

He caught a glimpse of himself in the full-length mirror mounted to the back of the bathroom door. The mirror was cracked and covered with stains; the maid service at the Exeter left as much to be desired as everything else about it. He set his cup down on the toilet lid and examined himself: not bad, he thought, thinner than he'd ever been, pale, in need of a haircut, but still a catch at thirty-five. He'd fallen far, there was no denying it, but he would rise again. He would put on a few pounds easily enough, get firmly back on his feet and face the day with a smile. It had been so long since he smiled.

He pushed the door in against the wall, tired of looking at himself and the things it made him think. He was too busy for idle thoughts. He had a plan to carry out and only four days left. The big opening at the art gallery was Friday night and here it was already Tuesday morning. All those fancy people coming to the opening of The Next Big Thing, the next *artiste* destined for fame. Some shutterbug, another photo-auteur, as if the world wasn't overrun with people taking pictures on iPhones and calling them art. The picture he had in mind for them, the centerpiece, would not be an image at all but the real thing. Three-dimensional, sensory stimulation at its most unimaginable. Performance art they would be talking about for the rest of their lives. He'd bought a digital camera just for the occasion, the kind that makes video recordings, too. The internet was flooded with stupid videos from stupid people who thought dancing kittens were the best thing ever, or their stupid babies laughing at nothing while they recorded them and put them online, hoping to end up on some idiotic morning show. The next must-see, the next YouTube sensation! Boy, did he have something for them to watch ... very soon. It had taken most of his meager cash to buy, but once it was finished, once he had released it into the world, he would be complete and not in need of anything.

He finished making his coffee with the lukewarm water from the sink, stirred it with his finger, and walked back into the hotel room to work out his itinerary. His planning had been meticulous so far, and now more than ever he must focus, focus, focus.

Chapter Fourteen

TOKYO PULSE

K yle hurried across Ninth Avenue at 46th Street, carrying a bag filled with two medium coffees, a toasted bagel for himself, and a croissant for Imogene. He glanced to his left and saw the Hotel Exeter sign, visible from ten blocks away by virtue of an unobstructed view. He'd never been to the Exeter, or even known anyone who had, but the big red letters extending up above its rooftop provided a signpost, a way of orienting oneself in a city that can be very disorienting to the uninitiated.

He'd picked up the coffee at Cecil's, a bagel shop he'd been stopping at every morning since he first started working at Japan TV3 as Imogene Landis's personal assistant. Imogene was diminutive in body only: short, thin, with a brunette bob she somehow made fashionable, and an outsize personality that surprised many people coming from such a small woman. Tiny would be an apt description. But once she opened her mouth most people took cover, and the ones who didn't tended to be thick-skinned, since Imogene's language was more like pepper spray. She'd lost more than one job because of it, and had been on the verge of leaving this one just when the murders in Pennsylvania made her a hit on late-night TV in Tokyo. The show was called Tokyo Pulse, produced by Japan TV3, whose

English-language correspondents were in New York – all three of them – and whose bosses in Tokyo knew a novelty act when they saw one. She'd been their financial correspondent, interviewing C-level economists and talking about financial matters she knew nothing about, nor cared to. And then, death in the countryside. A gay resort. Murder, mayhem, and ratings that shot up like a rocket. Now Imogene Landis was as close to a star as someone on television at 3:00 a.m. in Tokyo can be. She'd even learned to speak enough Japanese to sound ridiculous in the occasional asides she did to camera. But mostly it was business, as she now covered the city in a segment called Straight Up New York. Crime, politics, some culture when she got lucky. But a headliner in any event. Imogene-san was a hit.

Japan TV3 was located on the third floor of CityScape Studios, which were really just a large office building converted to television studios in the 1980s. They were big, and they weren't much to brag about, but they generated considerable revenue for the building's owners. They were also home to some of the best bad television shows no one has ever heard of. The YouTube of shoestring budget broadcasting. It was saying something that JapanTV3 could have an entire half-floor to itself. This is where you'll find Kelly Gerson, national political reporter who only went from her apartment in Flushing to the studios and back and had never been to Washington, Michael W. Podesto (the middle initial was in his contract), who had taken over the financial beat when Imogene moved up and who was quite good at it, their boss Leonard "Lenny-san" Baumstein, who reported directly to the high-ups in Tokyo, Lenny-san's icy assistant Gretchen, and, of course, Imogene and Kyle. The operation was supported by a dozen quasi-producers and assistants, and felt most days almost like a real TV show. There was even a deal in the works to expand beyond the single Japanese cable channel where New Yorkers could see the program. Someday soon, they all hoped, viewers would be able to enjoy Tokyo Pulse in every major American market. Imogene believed when that happened she would be able to write her own ticket, after thirty years in the business.

The elevator opened and Kyle hurried to his cubicle. The train back from Inwood had been delayed in two separate stations, once for traffic and another for a sick passenger, and he was almost an hour late. He managed to slip his jacket nearly off when Imogene saw him. She had her own cubicle – the days of an office were long gone – and was reading over a script when she looked up at the sound of the elevator.

"The withdrawals have already started, Kyle," she said, referring to the coffee he brought her every morning.

"I'm sorry, I got stuck on a train."

Kyle handed her coffee to her and set the croissant on her desk, at the same time draping his jacket over the back of his chair. Even though they sat back to back, in identical cubes, there was no mistaking the two spaces: Kyle's little fabric square was decorated only with a few photos of himself with Danny, their two cats, Danny's parents and Kyle's mother. Imogene, meanwhile, had given her cube the royal treatment, a sort of presidential suite of office cubicles. There were framed photographs her of her smiling next to New York City politicians, some whose names Kyle did not know (any Councilman would do), as well as a signed letter of thanks from Former President Bill Clinton, an invitation to some official state dinner that she probably picked up at a flea market, and a photograph of an Emmy. Imogene Landis had never won an Emmy, but anyone stopping by her cubicle would not know that. One of her favorite truisms, true mostly to Imogene, was that "Appearances matter." She could be heard saying it at least once a week. It was lost on her that an over-decorated 5 x 5 foot cubicle spoke more of desperation than success.

"You're coming to the opening, yes?" Kyle asked. He'd been counting on Imogene to attend his exhibit at the Pride Gallery. While she wouldn't cover it for Tokyo Pulse (she had pitched it to Lenny-san but he deemed it not interesting to a middle-of-the-night Tokyo audience), she promised as Kyle's long time boss and friend she would be there.

"I've made dinner reservations a block from there, of course I'm coming!" she said. "Lenny-san is my date."

"Lenny's coming?" Kyle was shocked. Their boss was a sixty-ish, squat, barrel-chested, balding Jewish man everyone knew was gay but who had never come out. He had lived alone with his aging father until the old man passed away two years ago, after which Lenny moved from Staten Island to Chelsea, expecting no one to notice.

"I may yet get him to let me do a short piece," she said, referring to the opening. "A sort of 'Tokyo Pulse' reporter makes good' thing."

"I'm not a reporter."

"They don't know that. It's three o'clock in the morning there, for fuck sake!" She sipped her coffee and sniffed her croissant – an odd habit she had of smelling her food. "If you want to be successful – "

"Appear successful," Kyle finished.

"Absolutely. Appearances matter. Like this morning, it appeared you had either quit or just didn't care enough to be here on time."

Kyle sighed. She was ribbing him, but he still didn't like it.

"I had to talk to someone in Inwood."

Imogene set her script down. "Inwood? Above Harlem, that Inwood? What the fuck's in Inwood?"

Kyle frowned at her. She'd been asked several times by Lenny-san to watch her language. A few people in the office had complained.

"The wife of a woman who died a month ago, fell in front of a train.

Imogene's eyes lit up just a bit. "Or was pushed? Is that what you're thinking? There's a story in being pushed in front of a train. And 'wife of a woman' means gay, I like that."

"Oh my God."

"No disrespect, Kyle, but gay has been good to me. Pride Lodge sent my ratings through the roof in Tokyo. I'm just being realistic. It adds to the story."

"At this point there is no story. Just thinking. Connections."

"I can use some, it's been very dry here the last few weeks."

"What are you reading?" Kyle asked, looking at the script on her desk.

"Bor-ing. Lenny-san wants me at one of Councilman Danhill's townhall meetings on the Upper East. Have you ever been to one of those? It's all old people. Not that I have anything against them, I hope to be one myself someday and get a lifetime achievement award. But we're talking zoning shit, wheelchair accessibility shit, kill me now shit. How he thinks this kind of thing won't tank us is beyond me."

Kyle booted up his computer, hoping Imogene would head out to the field soon with her producer Caren. In an operation this small, producers were also camera operators, script writers, editors, and sometimes office supply buyers, although that generally fell to Kyle. (Gretchen had been an executive assistant for one senior manager or another for nearly forty years and did not order office supplies.)

"Now, a juicy strangulation in a hotel room, with a guitar string, no less, *that*'s a story," she said. "But it's a Philly story, and we're not in Philly, are we?"

Kyle was barely listening, trying to think how the murders of Devin and Shiree could be connected. The Gallery was the most obvious answer, but how, and why?

" ... this guy Richard Morninglight, did you read about that?" Imogene said, continuing to chatter while Kyle barely paid attention. The name got through to him and made him sit up, turn to Imogene, and ask her what she had just said.

"I said it has all the elements of a great story. Gay hotel in Philadelphia, artist on the edge of fame, a hustler nobody saw come in our out, and having his head nearly taken off with a wire."

"A wire."

"A guitar string. You really have to pay attention, Kyle, or get your hearing checked."

"Richard Morninglight?" Kyle was staring at her now.

"You know him?"

"No. Well, I met him, once, at the New Visions show."

Imogene waited for him to explain.

"It's the New Year show Kate Pride has every January, to showcase talent she thinks is on the verge. The show last January had a half dozen artists. Devin was one of them."

"Who's Devin?" Imogene asked.

Kyle waved her off, wanting to complete his thought. "Devin was one of them ... Richard Morninglight was another ... and Shiree Leone did the catalog. That's it! The New Year New Visions show. The Pride Gallery."

"I want an exclusive on this," Imogene said, having no idea what 'this' could turn out to be, only that she wanted the rights to tell it first.

"There may not be any story here. Maybe it's a coincidence. I mean, Brooklyn, Inwood, Philadelphia? I don't want to see something that isn't there. Where did you read about Richard Morninglight?"

"Where did I read about him?" Imogene said, as if Kyle had missed the assassination of the President. "Online, where the hell else? It was front page news."

By front page, Kyle knew she meant what had once been called "above the fold" when newspapers were still in wide circulation. Now that nearly everyone got their information from the Internet, it meant stories that were seen before the reader had to start scrolling down.

"Let me read about this," Kyle said, turning back to his monitor. "When's your townhall?"

"Half an hour from now. I'm just waiting for Caren, then we'll take the van. You wanna ride along?"

"I'll skip it, thanks. The excitement might kill me."

"Fine, I'm sure you have work to get caught up on, considering you were an hour late. But if there's any 'there' there in this New York-Philly killing spree ..."

"It's not a killing spree! Not yet. Maybe never. Just let me think it through."

"So think, Kyle, and if it's not a coincidence, if there really is a story here, I take it to Lenny-san while everyone else is still in the dark. Deal?"

"Of course," Kyle said.

Imogene began to quietly read her script, memorizing her introduction to the townhall segment.

Kyle turned back to his computer and immediately did a search for Richard Morninglight. He pulled up the first story he saw and began to read the sordid details of a murder in a hotel room ninety-five miles away.

Chapter Fifteen

MARGARET'S PASSION

Danny found himself in a quandary. For the decade he had worked for Margaret Bowman the two of them shared a trust few people have with another. Best friends. Couples. Occasionally a boss and her assistant. A mother and son. That had always been a sensitive matter for them both, since Danny's mother, Eleanor, was alive and well in Astoria, Queens. She was retired these past fifteen years, living comfortably in a row house on 28th Street with her husband, Big Bob Durban, also retired. Danny and Kyle had Sunday dinner with them almost every week. Eleanor, *Ellie*, was a strong willed woman, a good mother, but possessed of a certain jealousy when it came to her son. She didn't like having to share him with anyone, including Kyle, and Danny had been careful all this time not to speak too much of Margaret in front of her.

He'd kept his relationship with his two mothers distinct. There were things he told Ellie, and things he told Margaret, and each of them told him everything. So it was strange for Danny to be fidgeting at work Tuesday morning wondering what Margaret was withholding from him, and how to go about asking her. He had never had to pry information from her before, and as far as he knew she had never kept a secret from him.

Something had been going on for the past several weeks. Margaret's new lawyer Claude Petrie, while having been referred by the old gentleman he replaced, struck Danny as an odd duck. Maybe it was the way he avoided looking directly at you, or the perspiration that seemed always present on his upper lip. *Shifty* came to mind. And now he was bringing in two strangers to speak with Margaret. He had been mulling it over for days, not wanting to question her judgment, yet worried something might be wrong. She might be ill, or preparing in some other way to leave. He wanted her to know he and Kyle were there for her. If she needed care, there was always the spare room, though he doubted someone as proud as Margaret Bowman would submit to being looked after. He had to know what was going on.

Danny slowly climbed the staircase Margaret and Gerard had built behind the kitchen. There were only twelve apartments in the entire building, six on each of the two upper stories, including the Bowmans', with the restaurant taking up the entire first floor. The restaurant had been their one true love, aside from each other, and they had wanted to be able to come and go easily, at any time of the day or night, without having to go outside. The staircase was no secret, except to the city, from whom they had never sought or received the proper coding to build a staircase. At this point nobody cared.

Normally Danny would call up and tell Margaret he was visiting, but he wanted an element of surprise. He knew she would be there – she was always there, and when she went out, she used the staircase and left through the restaurant when it was open. He told Trebor he'd be back and to please seat any guests who came in. Patricia, one of three day servers, was already stocking. Lunch was still an hour away, there was no reason to think he'd be needed for the next twenty minutes, so he climbed the stairs and gently knocked.

He was startled when the door opened before his knuckles hit the door a third time.

"Come in," Margaret said, opening the door. She was wearing a powder blue dress with a white sweater, looking much as she would were she heading to dinner with someone. She was always dressed as if company might be coming – except for the house slippers.

"No call, Danny?" she said, referring to his habit of letting her know he was coming.

"I wanted to talk to you," he said. He followed her wave and sat at the kitchen table. A kettle, anachronistic in this age of coffee machines and iPhones, was just on the verge of whistling above a stove flame.

"Tea?" she said, shuffling in her slippers to the stove.

"Yes, please."

Margaret set about pouring boiling water into two cups and dropping in tea bags. Neither of them said anything until she'd brought the cups to the table and taken a seat herself.

Danny looked around the kitchen. He'd seen it a thousand times, and it always reminded him of his grandmother's kitchen. There was a permanently outdated feel to it. Not old, but out of time, as if from another era.

"Chloe tells me Claude was here again yesterday, with two men," Danny said finally. Unlike Claude, he looked directly at Margaret. She was no-nonsense, and would not expect anything but directness.

"Investors," she said. Just like that. "Money men. I quite liked them."

Danny didn't know what to make of it. Was this simply about her investments? Were they financial advisors? Why the secrecy?

"Do they handle your ... estate?" he said, uncomfortable with talking about things that might bring up her death, her will, or the fact she was now in her eighties.

"No, nothing like that." Now Margaret was the one who looked away. She was hesitant, embarrassed. Finally she turned back to him and said as plainly as possible, "I'm in trouble, Danny. I'm broke."

He was stunned. Margaret's Passion was a very successful restaurant in its fourth decade, in a city where restaurants came and went like tourists. He knew the numbers, he did the budget and the ordering. While his position was day manager, he really was the overall manager. He saw the receipts. The idea that Margaret was broke was like finding out someone who appeared perfectly healthy had a month to live.

"I don't understand."

"Of course you don't," she said. "You remember all the news last year about Rebecca Effron?"

"The Ponzi scheme lady? 'Bride of Madoff' or whatever they called her?"

"Yes, always clever, these news people. Well, she was very successful at making people believe she was successful. I was one of those people, Danny."

He knew where she was going with this and his heart sank.

"Just over a million dollars," she said. There was no other way to put it. She had given a thief her life savings and now it was gone.

"I see."

"I don't think you do, Danny. It was everything I had."

"But the restaurant ..."

"It does well, yes. The tenants are reliable for the most part. But I'm eighty years old! The margins."

He knew she meant the profit margins, on the restaurant and the tenants. There was very little for either. The tenants essentially paid for the taxes and upkeep, with some left over, and the restaurant provided Margaret's regular income. What she was telling Danny also let him know that it had taken Margaret and Gerard nearly fifty years to save up that money she had lost in a bad bet, probably the only bad bet she had ever made.

"I'm not a greedy woman," Margaret said, her voice now thick with sadness. "Not even much of a needy woman. But I'm old. I may want to go somewhere warm soon, while I still can, and that takes money. And even if I stay here ... well, I may not be able to keep living on my own, you understand."

Danny felt his throat tighten. The last thing he wanted to do was cry, and he held it in check as best he could.

"The point is I'm going to need help sooner rather than later. The management company does well enough with the building," she said, referring to the small company that collected rent and took care of the day-to-day maintenance of her property, "but I'm hardly a fit landlord anymore."

"You don't need to be," he said, quickly trying to think of alternatives.

"Messieurs Tierney and Gossett, the two investors, are interested in buying the building."

"What about the restaurant?"

"Well, Danny, the restaurant is *in* the building. But they've made me a most generous offer: the restaurant stays, and I stay, until I pass."

There it was again, Old Man Time coming for them all.

"I don't like it."

"I didn't expect you would, which is why I was waiting to tell you."

"How can you trust them?" Danny asked.

"It's called a contract."

Danny stood up. He began pacing the small kitchen, from the table to the stove and back. "I don't know, Margaret, it just feels wrong."

"You're letting your emotions make that determination for you. You'll be safe as long as I am."

"I don't care about being safe! I don't want to be safe. It's not about that. It's about your legacy. Gerard's legacy."

She sighed and put her teacup down. "Dead people do not care about their legacies."

"What if I had a counter offer?" he said, stopping in front of her.

"What does that mean?"

"Exactly what it sounds like, Margaret. What if I came up with a counter offer? I can't promise a million dollars, but maybe half that, for the restaurant. You keep the building."

She thought a moment. "I pay you well, Danny, but I don't pay you that well."

"It doesn't matter. You're not the only one who can find investors."

"I didn't find them. They found me."

"What?" Danny said, struck by that bit of information.

"They came to me, through Claude."

I see, Danny thought. Young, new lawyer Claude knows Margaret has lost all her savings, and just happens to know two characters looking for a building to buy. Danny began to notice an unpleasant smell.

"Just don't make any decisions," he said. "Not until I do some research. You've trusted me for ten years, don't stop now."

Margaret sat staring into her tea a long moment. Finally, she said, "Okay, Danny Durban. I have trusted you since the day I met you. I don't even remember where you were working …"

"The Lamb Rack, East 63rd Street."

"Yes, dreadful place, it didn't last long."

"Which you saw coming, and you offered me a job."

"Oh, yes, you're right. But I really offered it to you because I was impressed. You know that, don't make me flatter you again."

He blushed. "I won't. But I will ask you to please give me till the end of this week."

"That's when Kyle's show is. Aren't you busy enough with all that?"

"I'm never too busy for Margaret Bowman," he said. "Now, speaking of busy, it's lunch hour and I imagine people are arriving right about now."

Danny leaned down and kissed her cheek. He had several things to think about, important things. Who were these men? Who were these men *really*? And how was he going to save his beloved Margaret from her own mistakes without making too many of his own?

"I'll let myself out," Danny said, and he headed back downstairs, quietly pulling the door closed behind him.

Chapter Sixteen

LUNCH AT THE STOPWATCH DINER

You can't miss the Stopwatch Diner, with its colorful neon "Stopwatch Diner" sign, complete with a stopwatch in the middle, and its throw-back design that lets you know this is a diner, not some high-end, overpriced Midtown Manhattan eatery. It's also directly across from the Seventh Avenue entrance to Penn Station and just a half block from Macy's, which is where Linda Sikorsky was shopping and why she was late.

Kyle had been punctual, arriving at the diner's entrance at precisely 12:30. He'd walked from the Japan TV3 studio, a short stroll on a sunny April day. Spring was in bloom and it always rekindled Kyle's love for New York City. Once the summer heat kicked in with its humidity and its smells he would again think there were a number of places he'd rather live, but spring and fall reminded him what he loved about this place.

The restaurant was packed, as it always was for lunch. Kyle was led through the crowd to a booth and handed a menu by a hostess who seemed distracted, eyeing the customers, looking for the next empty table. No sooner had he sat down and started looking at the overstuffed menu than

Linda arrived. He saw her. The two of them waved at each other and were soon hugging before Linda slid into the booth. They hadn't been together since the Pride Lodge murders. They spoke on the phone every few weeks, and emailed every other day, but no amount of virtual communication can take the place of being physically near those with whom we share our lives.

"I like the hair," he said, noticing immediately she'd let it grow out. He also noticed a touch of makeup, something Detective Linda had done without until recently. He made no comment on it, unsure if she would take his notice as compliment or criticism.

"It was Kirsten's idea," she said. "The makeup, too. Or maybe her influence. 'Idea' isn't accurate."

"I wish she would have come."

"Me, too," she said, holding out her hand to show Kyle the small but sparkling diamond on her finger. "It's a friendship ring, not quite at the engaged stage. It's one of the things I wanted to talk to you about."

Kyle smiled. He and Danny had worn rings since their first anniversary. Back then they couldn't marry in their home state of New York, but it had been important to both men to wear rings as a way of telling themselves, and the world, they were a couple. Kyle did not consider them engagement rings at this point, they were well past that, but he briefly wondered if they would get new rings when the time for a ceremony came, or just slip the ones they already had onto each other's fingers.

"I have things to talk to you about, too," Kyle said.

The waiter came over, in the harried way waiters in busy diners do, and held pen to pad for their order. Kyle told him they needed a few more minutes, and off he went for a more decisive table.

"Please don't tell me it's about murder."

"Yes, and no."

"I'm on vacation."

"Death doesn't take a holiday."

"No, but Linda Sikorsky does. And it is Linda Sikorsky, by the way. 'Detective Linda' will be no more in a few months."

"That's impossible," he said. "You'll always be Detective Linda, even if you're working in a car wash. Now what's this about?"

"I'm tired of police work," she said. "I want to do something different. Something I'm doing because I care about it, not because my father was gunned down by some thug when I was eight years old."

Kyle listened patiently. He wondered how much of this was Linda's decision, and how much had been suggested, subtly or overtly, by the new woman in her life.

"I became a cop because my dad was a cop. You know that, we've had that conversation before."

Indeed they had, that conversation and many more. Kyle was the first person Linda told about the real estate agent she'd met at a New Year's Eve party, a party just four months ago. But what could he say about moving too quickly? Kyle had essentially moved in with Danny sooner than that.

"You're not listening to me," Linda said, seeing the look on his face.

"Yes, yes, I am. You want to do something else, fair enough."

"I've wanted to own my own business for years," Linda went on. "A vintage store, like this one in Doylestown I love. They have everything there, just everything, and it's a very successful place. Jenny, the woman who owns it, has already agreed to be my mentor. And I have a name: *For Pete's Sake*."

Kyle knew that Pete was her father's name. He started to comment that this wasn't quite the clean break she thought it was, then stopped himself.

"Wow," he said. "Friendship ring. Retiring from the police force – you are retiring, right? You're not walking away from a pension."

"Retiring. I've got my twenty years in come September."

"Good. Good."

"So okay," Linda said. "I'll give you this. Since I'll always be Detective Linda to you, what's your question."

"My question?"

"Murder. I know that's what you want to talk about."

"Right, well … it's two murders for sure, and one death, the cause of which remains undetermined, except that it was a subway train. How she got in front of it is a mystery."

"Ah, Kyle Callahan loves his mysteries," Linda said.

"I don't love them. I just feel compelled to solve them. I would be perfectly happy if no mystery ever presented itself."

"No, you wouldn't. If dead bodies didn't pop up, you'd go looking for them, and you know it."

The waiter came back, displaying some impatience this time, so they did him the favor of ordering lunch. He paid just enough attention to write the order down and scurried away.

With the waiter gone, Kyle said, "I was hoping I could convince you to do some sight seeing in Brooklyn this afternoon. Imogene's covering a town hall on the east side, then she's heading to Gracie Mansion for the mayor's press conference. She won't miss me."

"I wonder," Linda said. "Might Brooklyn be where one of these murders occurred?"

"I just want to ask around while the memories are still fresh. The news said no witnesses, but that's impossible in a city like this. People just don't always know what they saw. There's a coffee shop and an all-night laundry near where Devin – that's one of the victims – was killed. I scoped it all out online, easy to find, won't take long, and I could show you were I used to live in Carroll Gardens."

"I don't know, Kyle. You have a show opening on Friday, isn't that what you should be focused on?"

"I think stopping a killer is more important. If all these people are connected, there may be more to come. I can't take that chance."

She thought about it a moment. "Fine, it's been thirty-five years since I was in this city and I've never seen Brooklyn."

"Excellent," Kyle said. "Next stop Brooklyn."

With their afternoon plans set, the two of them caught up over lunch. Linda became more animated as she told Kyle about the woman in her life, her mother's reaction, what was different for her now that she had come out to her colleagues on the New Hope police force. It was as if they were continuing their last phone call, but this time with the added pleasure of seeing each other across a small diner table. For the next twenty minutes there was no talk of killers or motives, whys or whens or hows, just two friends cementing a relationship they both knew would last a lifetime.

Chapter Seventeen

Lunch at the Stopwatch Diner (Meanwhile)

L inus Hern disdained diners, and the Stopwatch was no exception, with its ridiculous watch theme and the cheesy racecar flags on the wall. It may well be at the top of the list, if he'd had any reason to keep a list of pedestrian, crowded, loud, cheap restaurants that barely earned the name. The city's "A" rating on the window was meaningless — falafel stands had them in New York City, *bars* for godsake, and who with any sense eats in bars? The same people who eat in diners, he thought, barely listening to the weasel lawyer sitting across from him. He didn't like Claude Petrie, but he found him useful. It was Linus's overriding criteria in his relations with other human beings: they were either useful to him, or they were not. Some had the potential to become useful; those who would never be had no claim to his attention, and got none.

"She only knows that Jay and Victor are kind-hearted investors with her best interest in mind," Petrie said, referring to the two men who had convinced Margaret Bowman to sell them the building and everything in it, including her restaurant.

"Second only to theirs," Linus said. "She's no fool, so be very careful, we've almost closed this deal. Do not underestimate her ability to see you for who you are, Claude. Don't go around too often, you might spoil the ruse."

Claude was once again fidgeting in the presence of the restaurateur. He knew condescension when it was being heaped upon him, not to mention contempt, but he had been in a tight spot for some time and was in no position to tell Linus Hern to drop dead. *Please, right now, in this tacky diner.*

"You know," Linus said, sipping his coffee, "I'm curious why you've been the Judas in this, why the betrayal."

Claude stared at his fork, keeping his gaze away from the man across the table. "I don't ... it's not really ... we're not friends, Margaret Bowman and I."

"So she doesn't know about your little gambling addiction. The one you'll be able to pay off when this is over, providing you don't just spend your generous fee at a poker table."

Claude's face flushed with embarrassment. The truth of what Linus had just said was painful for him. He'd had a gambling addiction for years and it had cost him dearly: his wife, his co-op on the Upper East Side, the affection of his two teenage daughters who lived with his mother and had been trained to think as poorly of him as she did. The old lawyer Evans, Margaret's attorney for decades, had not been the best judge of character. He had not seen through Claude. It was another source of shame for him, to be taking such egregious advantage of a favor done him by a dead man. But he owed nearly a hundred thousand dollars, much of it to people who would soon be asking for his life if he couldn't give them his money. Money he didn't have. Money Linus Hern was paying him to deceive and defraud the old woman who lived above the restaurant named after her.

"I just ..." Claude half-said, trying to regain his composure.

"Yes?"

"I just wondered, why you're so determined to get her out of that building."

"Oh, its not her," Linus said. "It's her restaurant. Specifically, the man who runs it."

"Danny Durban?"

"Yes, Danny Durban. The one and only."

Claude could see Linus's face darken, the lids of his eyes lower slightly as hatred slid over his face like a veil.

"What did he ever do to you? It must have been terrible."

"It was, Claude, terrible. But that's not your concern, is it?"

Claude had never seen Linus Hern taken by surprise; it was quite a sight, like watching a supremely confident man slip on the sidewalk and land in a puddle.

"Are we about through here?" Hern said briskly. "I think I just felt a cockroach run across my foot. When will she be signing?"

"I'd say another couple days, maybe a week."

"A week?" Linus said, displeased.

"She's asked me to have Tierney and Gossett meet with Durban."

Linus nearly choked, his face reddening in the time it took for Claude to say those names, names that should never have been spoke in the same sentence.

"No, no, no," he said. "That's not going to happen. When did she ask for this?"

"Just before I came here. It seems she told Danny Durban about the sale and she wants them to meet."

Linus was fuming now, in a most dangerous way, his anger tightly controlled. His left eye started to twitch, and he set his coffee cup down to hide the tremble in his hand.

"You've failed me, Claude."

"Excuse me?"

"I am about to, yes. This could ruin everything. I'll have to speak with Jay and Victor. They'll need to be coached, quickly. I don't think all is lost, but things are very much in jeopardy now. Not only is Danny Durban sharp, but he has motives of his own."

"But he loves the old woman."

"Precisely!" Linus hissed. "Love is the greatest, strongest, most driving motive of all. Why do you think I'm so determined to destroy him?"

Claude knew then that Linus had been deeply hurt, somehow, at some time, by Danny Durban. But the two of them, together? Claude couldn't see that in a million years. No, it was more complicated than that, more involved. And complicated could work to his advantage. Linus Hern wasn't the only one with leverage. His hatred of Danny Durban and his mission to harm him could be used very effectively in Claude's defense. All was not lost after all.

It was then, as Linus tried to calm himself and Claude schemed to safeguard his payment, that Kyle Callahan and Detective Linda Sikosrky made their way past them to the exit. Kyle glanced over and did a double-take, wondering why Margaret Bowman's lawyer would be having lunch with Linus Hern, and for that matter why Hern would be eating at a place like the Stopwatch. From everything Danny had told him, Hern would never be caught dead in a tourist trap diner. He made a quick mental note of the sighting and herded his visitor to the exit.

Linus Hern never saw Kyle pass by. He was too busy thinking how to keep his plans on track. His partners would have to meet with Durban, if that's what Margaret Bowman wanted, and they would have to keep the deception going. Just a few more days, it could be done.

"Stay calm," Linus said, wiping his mouth and setting his napkin down. He stood up from the table.

"That's it?" Claude squeaked. He was startled that Hern would simply get up, without any indication the meeting was over.

"Yes, and no, my dear attorney, although you would never be mine. If we succeed, you'll be able to pay your debts and have enough left over to start the entire sordid cycle anew. But if you fail," and he leaned down, speaking inches from Claude's face, "if this mission fails because you tipped our hand, or the sweat on your upper lip gave you away … well, Claude, I know some of the people who want their money back from you. It would be easy enough to tell them they won't be getting it."

Claude felt his throat go dry. Linus Hern did not make idle threats.

"Now, if you'll excuse me," Linus said, "and even if you won't. I've stayed in this rat's nest of a diner long enough. Don't call me again, Claude. I'll call you."

With that, the tall, dark, brooding man named Linus Hern strode out of the restaurant, his heart nearly as heavy as his determination for revenge. He left the check on the table for Claude Petrie to pay.

Chapter Eighteen

BROOKLYN BOUND

The N train was among the more sprawling subway lines in New York City, spanning three boroughs from Queens, through Manhattan, and into Brooklyn all the way to Coney Island. It had held a place in Kyle's life since he first moved to New York. He had ridden this train from his longtime home in Carroll Gardens, Brooklyn, transferring from the F, for most of his working life in the City. And then for the last six years with Danny, the two of them rode it the opposite direction, into Astoria most Sundays for dinner with Danny's parents. It was also among the lines that were both underground and overhead, snaking up after a ride beneath the East River to travel along elevated tracks where it finally came to an end at Ditmars Boulevard. You could ride the N for well over an hour, and some people did: homeless men, women and the occasional child; curious tourists, the kind with backpacks and ragged, stained maps; cops, undercover cops, and the opportunistic thieves who could spot them through a crowd. It was one line among many in the spider's web of the New York City subway system, a marvel acknowledged to be among the best in the world. A public transportation miracle that was as easy to love as it was to hate.

Linda had never been in the subway. When she had visited Manhattan
with her parents all those years ago they had taken taxis and walked. Her
refusal to come to New York City meant she was as new to the subway
experience as a child, or as the many people who visited this place with no
desire to live here. She was trying to pay attention to Kyle, while marveling at the experience of riding the N train. They were on their way to
Brooklyn, where the artist Devin had met his end last Friday night.

"I don't know what I expect to find," Kyle said, and he noticed Linda
staring curiously at a street vendor transporting his entire shop rolled up
and roped on a hand truck. "Detective Linda? Are you listening?"

"Yes, yes," she said, turning back in her seat to Kyle. "You don't know
what you'll find but you're hoping to turn up something."

"Or someone, which would be better. There won't be anything to see
but a sidewalk that's been washed clean for days. But there are a *lot* of people around there. There are a lot of people everywhere in New York City.
Out in Astoria, where Danny's parents live, you can walk for six blocks and
not pass anyone, but there are row houses along all those streets, apartment
buildings, and for every one of them, eyes watching from the windows."

"Sixteen million."

"Pardon?"

"If you've got eight million people here, that's sixteen million eyes."

Kyle thought about it a moment. "God, that's creepy," he said, just as
the train pulled into the Prospect Avenue station.

The street vendor tilted back his portable warehouse and off they all
went, leaving the bowels of the subway for the afternoon sun.

Brooklyn has been around for over 350 years. Now one of New York
City's five boroughs, it began as a small Dutch-owned settlement in the 17th
century called "Breukelen." By the 19th Century it was a large, full fledged
city of its own, and was consolidated into New York City in 1898. Were
it still separate it would be the fourth largest city in the United States.
As it is, many people who live in Brooklyn consider it a world apart from
Manhattan. They live and love in enclaves like Prospect Park, Park Slope,
Williamsburg, Brooklyn Heights, and Kyle's home for twenty-six years,
Carroll Gardens. People who lived in the outer boroughs did not, by and

large, regret living outside Manhattan; by the same token, most people in Manhattan considered it, and it alone, New York City, and places like Queens and the Bronx might as well be Iowa. Some of those attitudes had changed after 9/11, Kyle noticed. Something about having the World Trade Center destroyed, with all those lives falling out of the sky into a pile of rubble and dead souls, united the city in a way it had not been before. New York City now meant *New York City*, with all of its sprawl and mess, and many more people were clueing into the advantages of living "out there," where rents were lower (not cheaper – nothing is cheap here anymore) and entire lives could be lived without ever setting foot on the Island.

Kyle was thinking of how long it had been since he'd taken the train to Brooklyn. Could it really have been since he moved in with Danny five years ago? He wanted to think he would not have so completely abandoned his old home, but it was probably true. There wouldn't be any reason for him to come here.

"What are you thinking?" Linda asked as they walked toward the building Devin had lived in. Kyle wondered if someone was going through the dead man's belongings yet, who had loved him, whose lives would be forever changed because of his murder.

"Nothing, just how long it's been since I've come here."

Kyle stopped them in front of an apartment building. "It must have been here," he said. "Somewhere around here. I found his address, that was easy enough, and the news said he was killed just a few houses down from where he lived, toward the subway. So here, somewhere in here."

Kyle stopped and looked around him: apartment buildings as far as the eye could see. And in those apartments, thousands of eyes. But would any of them have seen the killing, or the killer, and would any of them say so?

Linda glanced across the street and saw the coffee shop Kyle had mentioned. Sacred Grounds had been around for a decade, surviving the Starbucks onslaught with the support of a fiercely loyal neighborhood. "Maybe we should start there," she said, pointing at the shop.

"I think we have to. We can't knock on people's doors. You can't even get to people's doors here, you have to ring buzzers."

They headed across the street to the coffee shop. Linda noticed, two doors from it, the Laundromat Kyle had told her about: Fluffy Foldy's. Did the clever names ever end, she wondered.

Sacred Grounds had needlessly underscored its name with religious icons and paraphernalia on the walls, but clearly done in a post-religion, ironic sort of way: there was nothing overtly religious or spiritual about the place or the people who worked here, but the owner had thought it a good idea to hang replicas of Catholic relics and a dizzying array of saints, gurus, martyrs, and the obligatory photos of Gandhi and Mother Teresa. All to be gazed at while sipping a cinnamon dusted soy cappuccino stirred with a mint biscotti.

There were three disinterested baristas on duty when Kyle and Linda walked in. Kyle walked up to the front counter and was immediately told by a short, acned late-teen with a prematurely shaved head and a look of millennial disdain that, "The line starts there." He pointed at a sign that said exactly that, but there was no one waiting in front of them. The only other customer was planted by the window with a laptop and a headset to eliminate the sound of other life forms.

Kyle was hoping for some information from the child so he obliged him, shuffling backward to the sign, then, upon receiving a smile of approval, walking the few steps back to the counter. Linda did the same him, staying silent for now.

"I was hoping someone here was on duty last Friday night."

"You mean the night Devin was assassinated?" the barista said.

It was a strange choice of words, Kyle thought. "Yes, that Friday night."

"I told the cops everything I know already, which is nothing. I worked a double that day 'cause Pigpen has 'the flu' again, too much Tequila on Thursday night, and I was stuck here. It's not that busy on a rainy Friday, but busy enough that I didn't see anything, didn't hear anything, just saw it on the news the next day."

Linda leaned in, her hand on the counter. "So why would you say he was assassinated?"

"I have no idea why."

"She means, why would you use that word," Kyle said.

"Because it's Brooklyn, man! There's a government program to assassinate artists here, didn't you know that?"

"This is the first I've heard, thanks for sounding the alarm," Kyle said, wondering how such a delusional young man held down a job. "In the meantime, do you think your friends here saw anything?" He indicated the other two baristas who were multi-tasking with smartphones in one hand.

"Creamy and Soup?" the kid said, leaving Kyle to wonder if he'd spoken in code or those were their names.

"Yes. Creamy and Soup."

"Nah, they don't work nights, they're in school. Out to make something of themselves," he said derisively.

"Well, thanks for the information."

"What information?"

Kyle let it go at that and led Linda out of the coffee shop. Once outside, he said, "The kid's nuts."

"A diversity hire?" Linda said, smiling.

"Maybe. Like you!" and Kyle smiled, too. Linda's making homicide detective had been resisted by some on the New Hope police force who claimed she'd been hired just because she was a woman.

Kyle and Linda walked two doors down, turned in and found themselves at Fluffy Foldy's, the neighborhood Laundromat. Fluffy Foldy's matched its corny name with a corny interior, displaying photos, paintings, and one large mural of clowns. It seemed designed more for children than bored and impatient neighbors trying to get through one of life's most tedious chores.

There were a half dozen people in the place, several women of varying ages, one man Kyle pegged as gay the moment he saw him, and one old man who was sitting in a chair by the bathroom door, looking as if Fluffy Foldy's was his home during its hours of operation.

"So who are we looking for?" Linda asked.

"I don't know exactly. I doubt any of these people were here Friday night. It's too soon to be doing laundry again."

Kyle had begun to wonder what or whom he expected to find when he noticed a petite woman cleaning out a row of dryers. She was wearing the kind of mustard yellow uniform normally seen on hotel housekeepers. She was so short that he almost didn't see her as she bent into one of the large dryers and wiped it out with a cloth.

"Excuse me," Kyle said, heading over to her.

She pulled her upper body out of the massive dryer and turned to them suspiciously. Her hair was salt and pepper, heavy on the salt, and tied back in a long, thick ponytail. Her complexion was olive, Mediterranean, Kyle guessed, and she had intelligent, coal black eyes that he knew immediately missed nothing. She could be anywhere from forty to sixty; she had that kind of ageless look of some women of color who never seem to get older.

"Yes?" she said. "May I help you?"

"I'm hoping so," said Kyle. "What's your name?"

She stared at him with an expression that said her name was none of his business.

"This is Detective Linda Sikorsky," Kyle said, trying another tack. "We're investigating the murder that took place across the street last Friday."

Her eyebrow arched up – another policeman, this one a woman.

"My name is Yolanda," she said reluctantly. "I already gave a statement."

"Yes, yes," Kyle said, "and we are so appreciative of that. But Detective Sikorsky here just arrived from another jurisdiction, and, well, communication with the New York police has been slow. Could you just tell her what you told the other officers?"

Linda was impressed. Kyle had seen an opportunity to bend the truth to his advantage, with her in the middle, and had done it without a moment's thought.

"Just so we get our information in sync," Linda said to the woman. "A quick recap would be fine."

Yolanda thought about it for several long moments, and Kyle began to think she had seen through them. Then, she said, "I saw them. I was here that night. I'm always here. There is no one else."

"Oh, you own this establishment?" Linda asked.

Yolanda looked at her as if that was a preposterous idea. "No, I don't own it, I work here. Just me, and Willy who fixes the machines when they break. But he wasn't here. Just me. There is no one else."

"So what is it you saw, Yolanda?"

"I saw the dead man, he comes here to do his wash, or did, until ... He was walking toward the building he lives in – I see everything – and then he stopped and turned around. It was raining, but I could see the other man, the one who hurt him. They spoke, like they knew each other."

Kyle wondered how that would be determined, but he knew this was a woman who had been observing people all her life. Watching how they move, where they go.

"Then the one man takes the hood off his face, but I can't see from here, and he limps up to the dead guy ..."

"Limps?" Kyle asked.

"Yes, limps, but not like he was hurt, like he was born that way."

Kyle and Linda looked at each other. This was significant news. There was also something familiar about it to Kyle, but he couldn't think what at the moment. A tiny, faint bell had rung, and just as quickly gone silent.

"I have an aunt," Yolanda said, "She was born with a short leg. She walks like that."

Kyle felt his excitement rising. They had something as close to a description as they might find.

"The bad man goes up close to the dead one and ... makes him dead. I was in shock. I called 911 but it was too late."

"Did you try to help him?" Linda asked.

It was the only time Yolanda looked away from them. She had not gone across the street, nor had she told the 911 dispatcher who she was, or that she was calling from the Laundromat.

"It was raining," she offered weakly. "I thought they were, you know, kissing. It happens a lot."

"Yes, of course," Kyle said, leaving her to deal with her guilt another time. "This has been very, very helpful, Yolanda." He pulled a business card out of his wallet and handed it to her.

She read it. "You're with a TV station?" she said, alarmed.

"Japanese," he said quickly. "Nothing local, it has nothing to do with this. Detective Sikorsky can vouch for that. We're just following up on the investigation, and we thank you, Yolanda, we thank you so much."

Kyle took Linda by the hand, something Yolanda noticed and thought odd for policemen, and led them out of the Laundromat. Standing on the sidewalk, with Yolanda staring at them from inside, Kyle said, "Finally something substantial."

"A limp."

"But not just a limp. Something congenital maybe, or an accident of some kind. And it sounds familiar."

"You know this guy?"

"No. Yes. I've seen him somewhere, but I see thousands of people every day! Maybe I saw him in the subway and it stuck in my mind."

He recalled the man watching from across the street at the Katherine Pride Gallery. He hadn't seen him walk, so he couldn't say if he limped, but something told Kyle it was the man they were looking for, and if that was the case, he was getting much closer.

"I want to talk to Kate Pride again," Kyle said as they walked toward the subway. "Olivette Washburn – I'll fill you in on the ride back – said something about Kate being good to know if you were the one she was promoting, something to that effect."

"And you're wondering who it was she did *not* promote."

"Yes. If she chooses who to have at the New Year New Visions show, she must choose who she leaves out."

"A grudge."

"A deadly grudge," Kyle said, as they headed down the platform stairs to the sound of a train pulling into the station.

Chapter Nineteen

THE KATHERINE PRIDE GALLERY

orky Richards was alone at the gallery that afternoon. Kate Pride had been there throughout most of the morning, but had left for a late lunch with her husband, Stuart. It was a treat she allowed herself when she felt that everything was in order, as she did today. Kyle's photos were ready for public viewing, the two rooms where they'd been hung blocked off with velvet rope until the Friday evening opening. That left only the parlor, as it was called, for the other work they were showcasing. It was a small room, although large enough for Corky to have imagined many times how it might look as a studio apartment. Anything much bigger than a shoebox would make a suitable apartment in Manhattan, something of which Corky was painfully aware. He was currently staying in a dump in Coney Island with his cousin Patrick, and the commute itself had him longing for the day when he could find some cozy eighth-floor walkup with a Murphy bed and a hot plate within walking distance of his job.

It was a job he'd only had for two months. Corky Richards was new to the city, having migrated from Las Vegas less than a year earlier. The son of a showgirl and one of her string of boyfriends – she never bothered finding out which one – Corky had hated the desert heat and the garish lights, the vice that permeated everything about Las Vegas. And while it was certainly gay friendly, it was no place for a man like Corky to find a suitable husband, whom he would skillfully balance with a career that headed only upward. Was working the front desk at the Katherine Pride Gallery that career? No, but it aimed him in the right direction and put him in frequent contact with people he could step gently on as he made his way to the top. Some of the men even enjoyed being footstools.

He looked up at the sound of the bell ringing. Kate had not installed a door buzzer, the kind you have to buzz while waiting for someone to unlock the door. She considered it cold, and although this was an art gallery, nothing here was of great value. That was the whole point of the Katherine Pride Gallery: to launch those she found promising into the art world, where the next gallery would sell their work for much more. She was a talent scout, really, and a gambler. It didn't always pay off; some of the artists she had highlighted over the years had gone no further, while a few others had made good after their deaths from drug overdoses. And now Devin, of course, murdered. His works would immediately triple in value.

The man who entered the gallery did not at first look at Corky, but instead scanned the front room, the parlor, and the rope sectioning off the main gallery.

Corky, normally outgoing to a fault, chipper and always looking to network, remained unusually silent. Something about the man did not invite conversation. Part of it was the way he walked, with a shuffling limp that made Corky think not of a deadened foot but of a broken axle; part of it was his expressionless face, flat, almost reptilian, but very handsome. Corky was perplexed by the incongruity: a man with one leg that appeared to be twisted, walking as if his hips were out of alignment, yet the man himself was fit, good looking, even hot. Corky felt himself flush, and that thought, that annoying thought that flitted into his mind every time he saw a good looking man alone, buzzed into his head: Might this be the one?

"Good morning," Kieran said, walking up to the desk, still looking everywhere but at Corky.

"Good afternoon," Corky replied. He was strangely nervous, and he had the uncomfortable sensation of being exposed, even though the man appeared to deliberately not look at him.

"Yes, it is afternoon, isn't it? I stand corrected."

"I wasn't correcting you, that's not what I meant."

"No, I doubt you were." Kieran gazed at the roped off rooms. "It appears you've got something planned. An opening?"

"The rope, oh, yes. There's an opening Friday night. A photographer."

"A photographer."

"But we still have pieces available," Corky said, motioning toward the parlor. "We're not closed. What are you looking for?"

Kieran sighed, thinking a long moment. Finally he turned and looked at Corky. "Do you have anything by Devin? I think that's his name. Or Morninglight? Richard Morninglight?"

"Morninglight," Corky said, and he suddenly believed he knew the man's game. Obviously he was a buyer who read about the murders and was hoping to snap up something before the prices soared. What artist has ever been worth more alive than dead?

"We don't currently have anything of Devin's. We may never, actually. It's not like we're the executor of his estate."

"Oh," Kieran said, frowning. "Is he dead?"

Corky was confused, but only for a moment. He now thought the man was toying with him for some reason. You don't live to be a twenty-seven year old gay man, grown up in Las Vegas and now living in Coney Island, without knowing the games people play.

"Listen ..."

"How about something by Katherine Pride?" Kieran said. "Or isn't she dead yet?"

Corky felt the hairs on his neck rise. Something was wrong here, very wrong. "Kate's not an artist," he said.

"Does she have to be?"

Corky quickly rose from his chair. "I'm about to close up for lunch."

"So late? You must be starving."

"Yeah, well, I lose track sometimes."

"I'm sure you do. We all do."

"If there's nothing else ..."

"Oh, but there is, there is," Kieran said, smiling again. The smile made Corky nearly crumple. He wanted to be away from this man as soon as possible.

"I was hoping to speak with Katherine."

"Kate."

"If she prefers. Kate. Will she be here anytime soon?"

"Um, no, I'm sorry, she's out with ... the police, she's having lunch with some friends from the police force, they come here all the time. They keep an eye on the place."

Kieran turned and looked out the windows. "So they might be watching us right now?"

"I'm sure of it. By the way, I didn't get your name."

"That's okay," Kieran said, and he began to walk toward the door. "I'll give it to Kate myself."

Please, please let him leave, Corky thought, in as close to a prayer as he ever came.

Kieran turned back just as he reached the door. "We'll see you at the opening," he said. "You will the there, won't you?"

"Maybe. Listen, I have a boyfriend," Corky lied.

"As well you should, Corky. A young man as sharp as you, as fearless, really, I'd say the sky's the limit."

With that he turned back and left the gallery.

It took a moment after the door closed for Corky to feel himself relax. He hurried to the door and locked it, flipping around the hanging sign that said, "Back in 30 minutes!" He sat back down behind the desk and let his breathing slowly return to normal. It was only when he felt like himself again, a good five minutes after the man had left, that he realized he had addressed him by name. "*As well you should, Corky.*" But Corky had never offered his name.

The chill returned, and Corky sat for a long while rubbing his arms, trying to get the warmth back. What was that old nonsense his mother always said when he felt a chill? "Someone just walked over your grave." For the first time in his life he believed her.

Chapter Twenty

APARTMENT 5G

Kyle was in the kitchen preparing dinner for the three of them. Linda was staying in a hotel, which was fine with Kyle since it meant he wouldn't have anyone in the spare room until his mother arrived on Friday. Sally Callahan was usually the only guest they had during the year, but when anyone used the room Kyle would have to forego his morning ritual of working on his photography and scanning the Internet so as not to disturb them.

Linda was in the living room, talking on their landline to her new love, Kirsten. Kyle could hear her chattering away about her visit so far, their lunch at the Stopwatch, and the plans for the big opening night that Friday. She had not offered to have Kyle or Danny speak to Kirsten just yet, but Kyle suspected they would meet soon, and he wanted to. He would never dissuade Linda from being in a relationship, and he trusted her judgment, but he wanted to meet Kirsten as soon as possible, given she would become part of their extended family. Perhaps he and Danny would make a trip to New Hope in the summer, though not likely staying at Pride Lodge. As much as he wished them continued success, he would always associate the Lodge with the murder of his friend, Teddy Pembroke.

"You ready for the big night?" Danny asked.

Kyle jumped, sending speckles of spaghetti sauce across the stovetop. He'd been lost in his thoughts and hadn't heard Danny come into the kitchen.

"Well ... yes and no," Kyle said, quickly recovering. "I didn't want all this attention, you know."

"Of course you did. You take great photographs, Kyle. You wanted people to see them."

"They're on the Internet, anyone can see them!"

"I mean professionally. Artistically. The Katherine Pride Gallery is a big deal, and Kate would never be doing this if she didn't believe in you."

"Speaking of the gallery," Kyle said, about to bring up the dots he'd been connecting since his trip to Brooklyn.

"There's something I wanted to discuss," Danny said, interrupting him.

Kyle felt his heart sink. Danny did not often have things to discuss, and they were usually of a serious nature. Otherwise, they simply talked about things. "Discussing" them was on a deeper level, something reserved for grownups who needed to be very mature for the next few minutes. His immediate assumption was that something was wrong with Smelly. The vet would have called that day with the results of whatever tests they always insisted on doing. Was she sick? Terminally ill? He put the spoon down in a dish on the counter and turned to Danny. They could hear Linda on the phone in the living room, as alive as anyone newly in love.

"It's Margaret's," Danny said.

Kyle thought he said "Margaret" and that he was about to hear terrible news for the old woman they both loved.

"Is she alright?"

"She's fine," Danny said, realizing Kyle's misunderstanding. "Not 'Margaret.' Margaret's Passion, the restaurant." He took a deep breath. "I want to buy it."

Kyle didn't quite get what Danny was saying. He leaned back against the counter and waited for more explanation.

"She's in financial trouble. It's a very long story, but she lost all her money with that swindler who's been in the news."

"The Effron woman?"

"Yes, yes, Bride of Madoff and all that."

"Margaret Bowman lost her money? But she's so smart!"

"Smart has nothing to do with it," Danny said. "And it's beside the point. She lost her money, that's that. She's about to sell the building to these men, I've never met them but she's asked to arrange it. They're connected to Claude Petrie somehow."

"Claude?" Kyle remembered having seen him at the Stopwatch that afternoon.

"Listen to me, Kyle, there will be plenty of time for questions later. I just can't let this happen. Now I know we can't buy the building, but we could buy the restaurant. It would be enough to get her through, she's in her eighties for godsake."

"How much?"

"Do you love me?" Danny said. He slid up next to Kyle and put his arm around him.

"How much, Danny?"

"Five hundred thousand."

Kyle would have choked if he'd had anything to choke on. He heard the sauce bubbling on the stove, turned away from Danny and lowered the heat. He needed that moment to think of a response.

"We don't have that kind of money," he said quietly, knowing this is not what Danny wanted to hear.

"We can come up with half, I know that."

"That's our retirement money!"

"That we'll still have," Danny said. "It just won't be sitting in IRAs and 401(k)s. We'll see what it looks like, invested in one of the most reliable, loved, successful restaurants south of Central Park."

"Yeah, well," Kyle said, not convinced. "Where is the other half coming from?"

"Excuse me?" Danny said, having heard him perfectly well.

"The other half, Danny, where is it coming from?"

Danny grew quiet, weighing his words. "We have a visitor coming this Friday ..."

"You want to go into business with my mother! Are you out of your mind?"

"Not go into business," Danny said quickly.

"Everything all right in there?" Linda shouted, having heard the surprise in Kyle's voice.

"Fine," Danny shouted back, "We're fine. Tell Kirsten she can't let you come alone next time."

Kyle lowered the heat on the sauce and kept stirring, gazing into the pot.

"It's a loan," Danny said. "A silent partnership."

"Margaret won't let us borrow money from my mother to save her."

"Margaret doesn't have to know."

Kyle thought about it, stirring and stirring. Finally he turned the flame off. "We can ask her," he said, both resigned to it and dreading the prospect. He already knew she would say yes, but being indebted to his mother was not something Kyle ever imagined happening at fifty-five, and anyone who thought she would be a silent partner didn't know Sally Callahan. The only time she had ever been silent was the last few weeks when she refused to tell Kyle what it was she wanted to talk about. Now they would both have news.

"You might want to contact Claude if this deal is something you need to stop," Kyle said.

"I'll call him first thing in the morning. Margaret already reached out to him. She hasn't signed anything yet."

"Speaking of which, I ran into him at the diner. Not really ran into him, he didn't see us, but we passed his table. He was having lunch with Linus Hern."

Danny, who had relaxed after getting the hard part over with, was suddenly suspicious. "Linus?" he said. "I wouldn't have thought they even knew each other."

"They seemed to know each other well enough."

Danny filed the information away in the back of his mind, where he could turn it around over and over through the night: Linus Hern having lunch with Claude Petrie. Claude being Margaret's new attorney. What did Margaret know about him, really? Only what her trusted attorney Evan Evans had told her, and even someone as world-wise as Evans could be fooled.

Just then Linda called them from the living room. "Kyle, Danny! Come, come, I want you to say hello to Kirsten."

Kyle turned the burners off and the two of them headed to the couch, where Linda was holding out the phone.

"Who wants to be first?" she said.

Kyle and Danny exchanged looks, then Kyle shrugged and took the phone.

"Kirsten," he said, "We meet at last."

Kyle glanced at the digital clock on the nightstand: 11:30 p.m. He and Danny had engaged in one of their infrequent but luxurious rounds of sex, beginning with mutual massages. Neither of them had ever been highly sexed, and the comfortable sexual routine that many couples settle into after being together for years was workable for them. It made their sex life something to be savored, an expression of intimacy rather than frenzy.

Despite their weeknight sex, sleep had not come easily for either of them. Danny had been disturbed by the news of Claude Petrie having lunch with Linus Hern. It made no sense, yet the more he thought about it, the more it made perfect sense. He had wondered where these men came from, only a signature away from owning Margaret's building. He knew altruism was never a motive in business, and whatever promises they made could be broken with the right sleight of hand. And now, a connection to Linus. But for what? Was Linus Hern the man behind the curtain? There were many questions to pose, and Danny had every intention of getting answers to them. He managed to fall asleep thinking of a visit he would make to Claude Petrie in the morning.

Kyle stared at the digital clock and sighed, wondering if he would be able to drift off as well. He had his own obsessions, his own puzzle. He kept turning the pieces round and round in his mind: two dead artists and a dead graphic designer. Two clear murders and a third likely one. All of them connected to the Katherine Pride Gallery. And the man with the limp, who was he? It kept flitting about in his head. A glimpse of someone, a conversation overheard. He knew it centered on the New Visions show. He and Danny had gone to the opening. It was during the show that Kate

Pride had begun to pressure Kyle to have an exhibit of his own. Something small, she'd said. Just his work, not like New Visions, which highlighted a half dozen up-and-comers. The deaths were of people who had all been involved in that show. Were they being targeted? Were there deaths Kyle didn't know about? A list?

Feeling like he was onto something, Kyle quietly swung his feet off the bed, careful not to wake up Danny. Leonard, who slept between them, quickly uncurled and leapt to the floor, thinking Kyle was going to feed him, while Smelly just raised her head from the floor pillow she kept as a throne, glanced his way, and went back to sleep.

He'd put the show catalog back with the other books in the spare room. Flipping the light on, he hurried to the shelf. He'd been thinking too narrowly, only trying to identify Shiree Leone, the catalog designer. Now he realized the 20-page booklet contained the answers for it all: each death was connected to this particular show at the Katherine Pride Gallery. There had been six artists shown. Two of them were dead. Could this killer have them all in his sights? And was he one of the names left off, feeling his dreams thwarted by an arrogant art gallery owner who couldn't see his brilliance?

Kyle sat at his desk and flipped open the catalog. Leonard was at his feet, demanding tribute. Kyle absent-mindedly reached across his desk with his free hand, grabbed a few kitty snacks and dropped them on the floor. He ignored Leonard's pounce as he ran down the biographies of the artists: Devin, Richard Morninglight, Suzanne DePris, Javier Velasco, and a graffiti artist duo named Little Bit and Winter. He could check off Devin and Morninglight, they were dead. He'd have to quickly find out the status of the others. If they were alive, he could warn them. If they weren't, then his thesis would prove correct.

He needed help. With his job, and the show opening in a few days, his mother coming to town, he couldn't possibly accomplish everything by himself. He was going to call Detective Linda Sikorsky as soon as the hour was reasonable. She would have the rest of her life to run a vintage second-hand store and be happily married in New Hope. Right now there was a killer in Manhattan who was getting closer and closer, and the Katherine Pride Gallery was his bulls-eye.

Chapter Twenty-One

HOTEL EXETER, HELL'S KITCHEN

Kieran could see the massive, collective light of the city reflected in the clouds as he lay on the mattress staring out the grimy hotel window. Sleep was beyond him, a memory of something that had once been pleasant but had turned on him the last few months. Sleep was now dreaded almost as much as the dreams that came with it.

He stared up into the dark haze that hovered permanently over Manhattan once the sun had fled. New York City produced so much whiteness in the night sky he doubted anyone here had seen a star in years. The billions of tiny fires in the heavens could not hope to compete with the overpowering glare of neon, streetlight and a million apartments rising floor upon floor, their combined incandescence smothering the shine of God Himself. He knew how God must feel, too, overshadowed and forgotten. They were two of a kind, he and God. The difference, he supposed, was that he had no intention of slinking away to hide his impotence behind mystery. Kieran would not content himself with unanswered prayers from the vain and selfish. He would instead exact revenge and leave his name engraved with the great ones. All of New York City, and soon all the nation, would know his name. What the whisperers would make of him then wouldn't matter. They would be dead.

He listened as muffled sounds of violence echoed through the old hotel. In the month he had been living here he had witnessed little, but heard much. Groans of sex, shouts of rage, the occasional thud he assumed was a falling body. The police did not seem to care much what happened at the Exeter. They only showed up when someone was dead on arrival – or departure, as the case may be – otherwise leaving the denizens of the place to fend for, and devour, themselves. Junkies, drunkards, prostitutes and pimps, all roamed the halls here like living ghosts. They looked right through him, just as he considered them no more meaningful than the roaches he ignored crawling across his floor. The roaches would outlive them all and deserved more respect.

He would be glad to leave this place soon. Its decrepitude had begun to seep into his bones. He was used to the smells in his clothes, in the walls, in the people shuffling up and down the stairs when the elevator was broken, which was often, but there was another smell beneath them, the smell of failure, that he did not want clinging to him much longer. He had not failed; he had in fact succeeded most spectacularly. But if you stand in shit long enough, you will smell like it, and he wanted to be finished and gone before it could not be washed off.

Kieran watched in silence another hour as the sun began to come back, slowly pushing out the darkness. He liked the sun. Sometimes he believed he was the sun, so brightly did he shine. He and the sun together would chase the blackness from the sky and from his mind. Only his heart was out there beyond the edges of the void, broken and scattered and beyond healing. This suited him fine. He needed to be heartless now. Thinking on it, he rolled over, away from the window, and closed his eyes. The day had arrived and it was time to plan.

Chapter Twenty-Two

SUNRISE ON 8TH AVENUE

Kyle and Linda met for breakfast at the Sunrise Café in Chelsea, tucked between one of the ubiquitous nail salons that peppered the city and a neighborhood pet shop called Animal Nation that had weathered the neighborhood's changes for forty years. Chelsea had been known for half that time as a gay enclave, like San Francisco's Castro or Chicago's Boystown. It came about because the place had once been cheap, and bohemian types who could not afford Greenwich Village moved uptown just a few blocks to the once-industrialized Chelsea.

Chelsea took its name from the estate and house of retired British Major Thomas Clarke, who obtained the property in 1750. In time, factories arose in Chelsea, and the neighborhood still bears its working class roots; many of the buildings now housing million-dollar condos and impossibly high-end co-ops were once textile factories and 19th century sweat shops. By the 1970s the area had fallen on hard times … and along came gay people to begin its gentrification. As is the case with changing tides, they were being overrun and priced out by young couples with children, and Chelsea was now a mix with a decidedly healthy dose of gay, but a mix nonetheless.

The Sunrise was one of Kyle's favorite restaurants. It had only been in existence for nine months. Judging from the empty booths it may not make it another nine, but he loved the interior, with its exposed brick walls, the two old hutches they used to hold dishes, the slowly rotating ceiling fans. It had a rustic feel to it, as did the staff: older, with a whiff of country about them that made them seem out of place, yet very much at home, in the heart of one of Manhattan's most trendy districts. One of the waitresses, a buxom woman in her sixties wearing a white apron around her waist, had just taken their breakfast order and left with the menus.

Kyle had brought the catalog from the New Visions show with him and was running his fingers over the cover. "It's in here," he said. "The answers."

Linda had not complained about having her first visit to New York in thirty-five years turned into a hunt for a killer. She'd admitted to herself the first day that she didn't know what she wanted to see here, and had done nothing to prepare – no maps, no itinerary, no places of interest. Kirsten had encouraged her to lay it all out, or at least make a short list of sights to see, but Linda had told her no, she wanted to explore, to see it all before her as if she'd stepped into a wonderland and would decide to go left or right once the road was in front of her. But here she was in a café with Kyle Callahan, the two of them puzzling over a series of murders. Kyle and Detective Linda, an unlikely pair. She knew this is what she would rather be doing. She was not a sightseer, a shopper, a *tourist*. Maybe that would change when she and Kirsten went places, as they surely would. Paris had always been on her mind, and she'd never been west of the Mississippi. So many places to see, all the more reason not to think she had to spend her few days here running from building to building, must-see to must-see. She lived only two hours from here; those places could wait.

"What are you thinking?" she said, sipping the especially rich coffee the Sunrise served up.

"I'm thinking it's someone we won't find in this book."

She looked at him, puzzled.

"Someone who wanted to be," he explained, "but who was left out. Someone who missed the train to fame they think this is."

"And it's not?"

"For some, yes, but for just as many, no. To tell you the truth, Detective Linda, I don't aspire to be more than an amateur photographer. The show Friday is great, don't get me wrong, but it's not going to make me famous, and I don't want it to. But a lot of these artists" – and he tapped the catalog again – "this is how they measure their success, their value. It's who they are, and being left out, being rejected, is probably as life-changing as being in the show."

The waitress returned with their breakfast, each of them having three-egg omelets, toast and potatoes, set it in front of them and quickly left, realizing they were mid-conversation.

"I have to go to a luncheon with Imogene," Kyle said, as he slid his plate away and opened the catalog. "I need you to do two things. You're in on this with me, yes?"

Linda nodded, trying to look reluctant but knowing from the first words Kyle mentioned of a killer she'd be hooked.

"Good. I emailed Kate already and she's expecting you at the gallery. Two things: one, what became of the other artists in the show. Their names are here." Kyle quickly pointed out the names of the graffiti duo, the woman Suzanne DePris, and Javier Velasco. "And two ..."

"Whose names are *not* there."

"Exactly."

"Notice the plural, Kyle. 'Names.' What if we're looking at several people here? What if Kate Pride turned down a dozen?"

"We'll worry about that if it's true," Kyle said, closing the catalog.

Kyle looked at his watch and began to eat. He was running late again, but he knew Imogene wouldn't notice today. She was being honored at a luncheon at the Carlton Suites Hotel, a big deal for someone whose career had been on the wane just six months ago. She'd be consumed with how she looked and what she would say, should she find herself at a podium.

"Have you thought about women?" Linda asked, setting her toast aside.

"Not since ... ever, really," Kyle replied.

"Not like that, silly! I mean for the killer. Isn't it a little misogynistic to assume a man is doing this?"

"I don't think Richard Morninglight would make a sex date with a woman."

"What if he didn't know?"

Kyle was intrigued, but not convinced. The murders were too brutal, too personal. They had all the hallmarks of a very angry man. "One step at time. Let's narrow down the possibilities and see what's left."

Linda nodded. Her visit to New York City was turning out to be more than she'd imagined. It also reminded her of the things she loved most. Did she really want to walk away from the police force? Or could she do both? Could she run a store named after her father, *and* be Detective Linda? And what would Kirsten make of all this when she told her? So many thoughts turning around in her mind. She would have to shut them off and focus. Twenty minutes from now she'd be at the Katherine Pride Gallery, looking for answers and needing to think clearly.

"When do we get the police involved?" she said at last.

"They already are," Kyle said. "They bark up their tree, we bark up ours."

He winked at her then, not something that came naturally. His father had been a winker, and Kyle had no idea why he'd done it. Maybe his mother, and whatever she had to tell him – mercifully forgotten in the chase – had made him think of his father.

Kyle waved at the waitress for the check. "You finish," he said, seeing that Linda was barely halfway through her breakfast. "I'll get breakfast, you get yourself to the Katherine Pride Gallery. We'll meet after the luncheon. I'll text you the address."

Before she could say anything, Kyle took the check and hurried out. It wasn't being late he dreaded, but the list of things he knew Imogene would already be asking for. Timing was everything, and the timing right now could not be worse.

Chapter Twenty-Three

CLAUDE PETRIE, ESQ.

C laude Petrie's office was at the very top of the stairs in a fifth floor walkup on 41st Street a half block from the Port Authority bus terminal. The entire building smelled like exhaust from buses rolling in from the Lincoln Tunnel, endless lines of them that never seemed to stop. And if you stood on the fire escape, craned your neck out and looked south, you could see the Hotel Exeter. You could also fall to your death, as one burglar did two years ago when she slipped on the ice that had built up on the landing. Her body had gone unnoticed for two weeks; that's how long it took for the smell of decomposition to be stronger than the small of bus fumes.

To the right of Petrie's door, which had *Claude Petrie, Esq.* stenciled on it in chipped black letters, was a dentist who catered to Guatemalans and, to the left, an escort service whose escorts were sometimes seen but rarely heard. Young men for whom wages had remained flat over the last decade and whose appearance reflected the decreasing standards of the service that employed them. Claude had been careful, when under the tutelage of Evan Evans, never to meet here, lest they encounter one of the "models" or overhear an argument about compensation. His relationship with the old gentleman had begun as a favor to Claude's late father, who, like Margaret Bowmen, had retained Evans for many years. Noah Petrie had no idea his son moved in such seedy circles, and Claude had made sure it stayed that way until Noah's death, and Evans's three years later. It wasn't that Claude would not prefer an office on Central Park South or somewhere in TriBeCa, but this is what he could afford, and most of his clients were quite at home in this environment.

Danny stood outside the door wondering how long ago Petrie's name had been painted on it and if he would ever have it refreshed. He'd seen a short man who looked to be of Central American stock leaving the dentist's office with an ice pack held to his face, listening while an older woman hectored him as they walked down the stairs. Danny checked the business card Margaret had given him. While he was obviously in the right place, it just didn't seem like somewhere old Evan Evans would have spent time. Danny assumed Claude Petrie did the visiting.

After pressing the door buzzer and waiting several seconds, Danny was greeted by Claude himself. There was no receptionist, no receptionist's desk, and no one else in the office, which proved to be one room. A desk was in one corner by a window that hadn't been washed in thirty years. Behind it, a swivel chair that looked to be among the first manufactured. On the desk were stacks of manila folders, pieces of paper, two staplers, a phone, and a coffee cup being used to hold pens and pencils. Two guest chairs were in front of the desk; Claude motioned to them as he welcomed Danny in.

"Mr. Durban," Claude said, shaking Danny's hand. "I would have been happy to meet you at the restaurant."

"I enjoyed the walk," Danny said, in way of an indirect reply. "Gramercy Park to here, it's a good half hour in foot traffic."

"Indeed, indeed. Please, have a seat."

Danny sat in front of the desk and waited for Claude to take his place behind it. A long, awkward moment ensued as Claude leaned forward, his elbows on the desk, his hands clasped together, waiting for Danny to speak.

"I'm going to buy Margaret's Passion," Danny said finally and in a tone that did not make it a suggestion.

Claude looked at him a moment, then smiled. "I'm sorry, Mr. Durban, but that's already been arranged with Mrs. Bowman. I just have to take her the papers."

"She won't be signing them."

"I don't understand."

"It's not complicated." Danny leaned forward, close enough to make Claude uncomfortable. He pulled back from Danny, nearly sliding backward in his chair.

"I know who your investors are," Danny continued. "At least the one who matters, the one I'm sure is calling the shots. The one you're going to arrange a meeting with, for me, as a surprise. Linus Hern doesn't like surprises, this should be fun."

Claude had gone pale. He slumped in his chair, and even though the office was cool from the spring air coming in its one window, he had begun to perspire.

"I don't know where you're getting your information," he said, "but my investors' names are – "

"It doesn't matter who they are," Danny interrupted. "It matters who they're working for. We both know it's Hern, so we can stop this little game of cat and mouse, Claude. May I call you Claude? I'm the cat here, make no mistake about it. Margaret doesn't yet know what you've done or who you've done it with. I'd rather not tell her, it could do serious damage to your career, such as it is."

Claude had slipped into full panic mode. Margaret Bowman was very well known in this town, and very well liked. She could most certainly make his life more difficult than it already was. He flashed on himself being smeared in the daily papers.

"What is it you want?" he asked Danny.

"I want you to arrange a meeting with Linus, without telling him he'll be meeting me. This afternoon is fine, say … one o'clock? I can get Chloe to cover while I take my leave from the restaurant early. You know Chloe. She certainly knows you. Just tell Linus you have very important news about the deal with Margaret's Passion and you'll meet him at the Stopwatch for lunch."

Claude's eyes widened. How could this man know about the Stopwatch?

"He doesn't like it there," Claude stammered.

Danny smiled. "I'm sure he doesn't. So one o'clock it is. And the second thing, Claude, is that you'll be telling Margaret Bowman in a letter you won't be able to continue as her attorney. Very sorry and all that, but your workload has gotten just too much. An abundance of riches."

Claude almost laughed at the barb. He wasn't about to tell Danny Durban about his gambling debts or the shambles he'd made of his life. He knew that Linus Hern, too, could make things worse for him. He suddenly started thinking of places to go, destinations on a train route where he could stop anywhere and simply vanish. It was coming to that.

Danny stood up. "Don't worry about the contract with Margaret. My partner Kyle, his mother and I will be seeing another solicitor about that, but we appreciate the offer."

They hadn't yet spoken to Sally Callahan about investing in the restaurant, but Claude didn't know that, and Danny hoped by saying it he could make it so. He stood from the guest chair, declining to shake hands a second time.

"Good day now, Claude. I'll expect to see Linus at one o'clock this afternoon. I know he's very punctual. Not from experience, just from his character. Evil is always on time."

Danny knew he would never see Claude Petrie again and was glad of it. He showed himself out of the office, leaving Claude to wipe at the sweat running down his forehead. Much in both their lives had just changed.

Chapter Twenty-Four

TOKYO PULSE

"I haven't been in the top fifty in five years," Imogene said. "I'll take forty-seven. This is progress."

Imogene, Kyle and Lenny-san were gathered around Imogene's desk while she fretted over the luncheon she and Kyle were attending. It was an annual event recognizing the best of New York women in media. There had been a time in her career when she would have been in the top ten, seated near the lectern and busy signing autographs outside the banquet room, but those days were long gone. She hadn't even attended the luncheon for the past three years. She'd grown tired of being asked who she was and if she could please provide identification.

"Who's forty-six?" Lenny-san asked. "Probably that cow from Wander Women, what's her name?"

"Corrine," Kyle said, naming the woman who had managed to start a successful YouTube channel featuring New York women's travel stories. "Corrine Bradlaw."

Imogene started to say she remembered Corrine when she was just an intern at the local ABC affiliate where Imogene sat at the weekend anchor desk, then she realized it would date her and left it unsaid.

"It doesn't matter who's number forty-six, forty-eight, or number one, really, we're all in this together. Is that what you're wearing?"

Kyle looked down at himself, sitting in his chair. He'd worn his usual work clothes: khaki slacks, a button-down shirt with the sleeves rolled up above his wrists. "No," he said. "I have a suit in the closet for these things."

"Thank God. You're my assistant, Kyle, appearances matter."

Lenny-san nodded, knowing all too well the truth of it. At sixty, he appeared to be what he was: the manager for an obscure, often cheesy, Japanese cable show that prided itself on including segments from America, produced as cheaply as possible. He also appeared to be forty pounds over-weight, short of breath after walking across a room, and in need of a good teeth whitener. Leonard Baumstein had been in the business even longer than Imogene Landis. Their paths crossed often over the years but he had never expected to be her boss, which in this case meant joining her near the bottom of the media barrel. He considered himself a short timer now, with only two more years until he could start collecting social security to supple-ment his various 401(k)s. Then he could take a cruise every summer and spend his days reading autobiographies. Life at the bottom could be good, or at least good enough for Leonard Baumstein.

"I gotta make some calls," Lenny-san said. "You look great, Imogene. And congratulations. You get, what, a plaque or something?"

"A certificate. Without a frame. These bitches are cheap."

"Well, if anyone deserves a certificate without a frame, it's you," he said, and he turned and headed into his tiny office.

"I might have a story for you after all," Kyle said when Lenny-san was gone. His tip on the Pride Lodge murders had resurrected her career and gotten her off a financial beat she hated. It was the story that all late-night Tokyo had talked about for a month, and was entirely responsible for her making her number forty-seven out of fifty named in today's event program.

"More murders I hope," she said. Then, realizing the insensitivity of it, "As long as no one gets hurt, of course!"

"Of course. No one gets hurt, just killed. Don't worry, dead people don't care what you say about them. But I get it. It goes with this business.

I've run into that with my photography, finding myself in the position to taking a photo of something I think I shouldn't."

"Like that guy who got a shot of the man on the subway tracks, just before the train hit him. Gruesome. But great front page."

"Yes, like that. It's a fine line sometimes. I felt bad about poor Teddy dead at Pride Lodge, but he was gone and someone was going to tell the story."

"So what's the big mystery this time?" She swiveled around in her chair to face him.

"I'm not sure yet, but several people connected to the Katherine Pride Gallery have been killed, and more may be on the way. Which reminds me, I need to make a call."

He took his cell phone and stood up. He had a landline but making personal calls in an office cubicle always made him self-conscious. Everyone pretended not to be listening when they were.

"I'm looking forward to your opening Friday," Imogene said. "Lenny-san caved, I'm doing it as a gritty art world after dark piece. The Tokyo audience won't know there's nothing gritty about New York anymore."

Kyle felt his stomach lurch. He had hoped Imogene would abandon the idea of covering his exhibit. It wasn't news, and the Tokyo kids who so enjoyed laughing at Imogene (something she had never been told but that Kyle knew was among the show's main attractions) would probably find it pointless. But he loved Imogene and Imogene loved him, and she had dogged their boss to do a short piece about the gallery show. Now she thought it might tie into some murders and get her another salary bump, maybe even a better offer.

Kyle excused himself and walked into the station's kitchen. It was barely large enough to hold a table with six chairs, a microwave, and the Keurig machine Kyle had bought with his own money. He was a K-cup fanatic and even traveled with their least expensive model. The kitchen was usually empty mid-morning. He walked over to the window where he could look west toward the Hudson and called the familiar number on his speed dial.

"Linda here," the voice said, answering on the second ring. "You need to unblock your phone, Kyle. You're one of only two people I know who still has a blocked phone. It might as well read 'Kyle Callahan' when you call."

"I'll get around to it," he said. "In the meantime ..."

"In the meantime I'm waiting, Kate's running late, it's just me and the desk guy."

He heard Corky correct her in the background.

"Corky," she said, "more than a desk guy, very available for the right suitor. Does anyone say 'suitor' anymore?"

Kyle could imagine her rolling her eyes as she said it. "Listen," he said, "I just thought of something else."

"The limp."

"Yes! How did you know? And please don't say 'elementary.'"

"It just makes sense. Maybe she turned down a dozen people for the show, but I'd bet only one of them walked funny."

Kyle heard more chatter from Corky.

"Oh, sorry. I'm told I shouldn't say 'walked funny.' People who walk funny might be offended."

Kyle smiled. He knew there were things about living in a culturally sensitive world Linda needed to learn, or that, being Detective Linda, she might reject out of hand, like fretting about language when lives were at stake.

"I'll remember to ask about the man who walks differently," she said, "and soon. Kate just pulled up in a taxi."

"I'll let you go then. No phone calls until the lunch is over, but text me, I'll keep it on vibrate. Meet me outside the Carlton Suites at 2:00. If it's not over by then I'll leave anyway."

Kyle clicked off, wishing he could be there with her. The last place he wanted to be was a luncheon listening to Imogene whisper criticisms of the forty-six women ahead of her.

Chapter Twenty-Five

THE KATHERINE PRIDE GALLERY

Corky pegged the woman as lesbian the minute she entered the gallery. Kate Pride had not told him to expect a Detective Linda Sikorsky, so when she walked through the door as if she had something terribly important to discuss with Kate, he switched to full screening mode. Filtering was part of the job; Katherine Pride was well known in the art world, especially its cutting edge, and plenty of artists tried to get their portfolios to her through improper channels. Pretending they were there for some other reason was a favorite and transparent ruse. It was like impersonating a doorman to give Taylor Swift a CD of your material as she stepped out of a limo. Corky was not easily fooled, and would have none of this "I have to see Kate Pride right away" business. Besides, information was power, and screening people who insisted they had booked time with Kate was one of his best ways of staying informed. To be informed was to have leverage, New York City's most valuable currency.

Linda was patient by nature. It was a necessary trait in homicide investigation; you often had to wait for evidence to present itself, or wait for test results, or simply wait for someone you were questioning to stop crying and give you an answer. But even someone as calm as Detective Linda could lose it when faced with an obstacle like Corky. He didn't seem to hear her when she said she needed to speak with Kate Pride right away. He began asking her where she was from and with whom she had made this alleged appointment. She told him she was a friend of Kyle Callahan's, the photographer whose photos were on the walls, for godsake, and that the matter was urgent. He stalled some more, and Linda realized he was pumping her for information. Finally she pulled out her badge, something she refrained from doing outside her job unless it was absolutely necessary.

"I'm a homicide detective," she said, holding out her shield. "New Hope Police Force."

Corky's eyes widened. This was definitely prime information. He felt his Twitter finger twitching already.

"Is this about Devin?" Corky asked, staring up at her.

"I'm not at liberty to say."

"Where's New Hope? Isn't that California?"

Linda sighed heavily, wishing someone had told this young man she was coming.

"Listen," Corky said. "I don't know if it's related, but there was this guy in here yesterday, really creepy. We never met but he knew my name, weird, huh?"

Before Linda could respond the phone rang. She saw it was Kyle and had a quick conversation with him that Corky interrupted to tell her he was not "the desk guy" and to poo-pooh her use of the words "walked funny." She was about to slip into the parlor to escape the presumptuous young man when she saw Kate Pride pull up in a taxi and ended the call.

Moments later the door opened and Kate Pride came in, an oversized leather purse hanging from her left shoulder. She had a binder in her right hand that she handed to Corky when she got to the desk.

Corky took the binder without a word and said nothing more. Kate was the boss, and as much as she liked Corky, she had no patience for his prying. He was a very young man with a lot to learn; she was happy to teach him what she could, but on her terms and in her time. This was not one of those times.

Linda shook hands with Kate. "Linda Sikorksy."

"Kate Pride."

"Is there somewhere we can talk privately?" Linda said, glancing at Corky.

"Yes, certainly, I have a small office in the back."

Kate led Linda to the back of the gallery. "Can we get you something?" she asked as they left the room. "Coffee? Water?"

"I'm fine, thanks," Linda said, disappointing the eavesdropping Corky. When Kate asked if 'we' could get her something, she meant Corky, and he was hoping for the chance to scurry to Breadwinner's across the street, get some coffee or scones, and insert himself at least one more time into the conversation. Now he had been effectively shut out, and he started brooding. It took Corky all of ten seconds to switch from aloof to brooding, excited to brooding, any mood at all to brooding; if he was born to succeed, as he often insisted, he was equally born to brood.

He turned his attention to the binder. It was filled with photographs for the next exhibit. Kate was always three steps ahead. The photographer Kyle Callahan would have his moment in the sun, and within a few weeks there would be another one. A sculptor this time, Corky could see as he flipped through pictures of the woman's pieces. Women sculptors remained a significant find in a medium still dominated by men. The most famous ones tended to be potters, but this woman, Geraldine Wenzel, did absolute wonders with heavy metal. Corky quickly forgot about the detective from California and the strange limping man and his horrible landlord harassing him for back rent, as he glanced at the amazing sculptures that would soon be placed around the Katherine Pride Gallery. So short was his attention span that he did not notice the same limping man watching him from Breadwinner's as he enjoyed his last meal in New York City. Had the good detective asked for coffee, things might have turned out very differently. Corky would have gone across the street and seen the man he had tried to tell her about. But that is the dark side of serendipity. One man's happy coincidence is another man's misfortune. Bad luck appeared to be on a roll.

Chapter Twenty-Six

THE STOPWATCH DINER

Danny arrived at the Stopwatch twenty minutes early, knowing Linus would not be late. He took a booth facing the front so he would be able to see Linus before Linus saw him. He wanted to observe the look on Linus's face when he realized Claude was not the one waiting for him.

The bad blood between the two men went back a decade. Danny had first met Linus when he began working at Margaret's Passion and Linus had dinner there one evening with several companions. He'd stared at Danny throughout the meal and at first Danny thought it was flirtatious; but then he sensed hostility in the restaurateur's gaze, and finally something close to hatred. A hatred he had never understood, but that had become almost mutual. 'Almost,' because Danny was not the hateful sort, but he had witnessed enough destruction brought about by this venture capitalist to come close to hating him. *Despise* would be a better word. Linus left victims in his wake, starting up restaurants with an investor or two, then selling to some hapless dreamer and making off with a nice profit. More often than not the restaurant failed within a year, and the poor owner and his backers, who were usually family members, were left holding an empty bag while

Linus was off to the next start up. That was his specialty: starting up, then leaving. He never stayed for the unhappy endings.

"You want a warm up?" the waiter asked, nodding at Danny's coffee cup. He hadn't seen the man scurry up to him, coffee pot in hand.

"No, I'm fine," Danny said.

He looked over as the waiter disappeared and saw Linus Hern enter the front door. Hern scanned the restaurant for Claude Petrie, and after a few moments of puzzlement – he was not one to be kept waiting and knew Claude would be punctual – his gaze landed on Danny and he froze. He cocked his head, not sure if this was a chance encounter or if Danny was the one he was here to see.

Danny nodded: yes, Linus, I've been waiting for you.

While not exactly going pale, Hern's face fell even further than its natural frown. He brushed past the maître de and walked to Danny's table.

"I'm assuming Claude's not coming," Linus said.

"You would be correct," Danny replied. "Please, Linus, have a seat."

Hern hesitated and considered leaving, then decided the only way out of this situation was through it. Now that his plan had been found out he would have to sit and get it over with. He slid into the booth across from Danny. No sooner had he settled in than the waiter reappeared.

"Go away," Linus said to the man, who'd had his share of rude customers and did not take it personally. He shrugged and shuffled off to another table.

"So. Danny Durban. I never anticipated this, if anticipation is the right word."

"I think it is for you, Linus. The sweet anticipation of deceiving Margaret Bowman. She just turned eighty, but you know that."

"Yes. I remember her birthday luncheon. I wasn't invited."

"Don't worry, you're on the list for her hundredth. Where was I? Oh, yes, tricking an elderly woman into signing over her building, in which both she and her very successful restaurant reside, only to find herself out of a home in a few months and that restaurant closed. Am I right? Did I get the plan down?"

"Close enough. But the eviction part's off. I would never put someone that near the end of her life on the street."

Danny sighed. He was tiring of the man already. "What I don't understand," he said, looking at Hern now as if examining him for his many imperfections, "is why Margaret? Why an old woman who has run a restaurant for thirty years? She's not defenseless, but obviously vulnerable. Here mind's not quite as sharp as it used to be, or she would have seen through your hired guns the moment they walked in the door. I'm sure it was Claude who told you about her financial problems, and there you were, like a snake that had lain patiently in the grass all this time."

Linus thought a long moment, considering his reply. "It's not Margaret," he said, leaning across the table, inserting himself perilously into Danny's personal space. "It's you."

Danny couldn't help himself; he pushed back against the cushion wanting to distance himself from a much too close Linus Hern. Finally Linus eased away, the hint of a smile coming onto his face.

"Me?" Danny said.

"You really didn't know, did you?" Linus said, waving over the waiter. "I'll have that coffee now."

Linus took the time they waited for his coffee to be poured to gather his thoughts. He felt a sudden peace come over him, if peace can relieve a malevolent man. He put creamer into his coffee, stirred it slowly, and carefully set his spoon down on a napkin.

"It's a very short story," Linus said finally. "I was in love once, very much so. He was younger than I, about ten years. Sal was his name. Salvatore Minelli." He looked at Danny, waiting to see any indication the name meant something to him. "No," he said. "I suppose you wouldn't remember him."

Danny had become intensely uncomfortable, regretting the meeting. He should have done it formally, in the company of witnesses, or in a letter, anything that would have given him distance; but it was too late now, Linus was at this table, in this diner, and he had no choice but to hear him out.

"Anyway," Linus continued, "he was the only man I've loved, really. Certainly the only one for whom I've ever let down my guard. I honestly believed we'd be spending the rest of our lives together. Me, a successful restaurateur, Sal the manager of a very popular Gramercy Park restaurant."

Hern watched Danny again, and this time something clicked.

Danny felt his stomach lurch. He did remember the name.

"I have to correct myself," Linus said. "A moment ago I said this was not about Margaret Bowman, but it is. It's about Margaret, her restaurant, you. All of it. You see, Sal was on the fragile side. It's one of the things I loved about him. I was hard, he was soft. I was the storm, he was the calm. And one day he got fired from his job, for reasons that were never clear. It seems the old woman who owned the restaurant had found someone she preferred, someone she favored and has favored ever since."

Danny knew now, he remembered. The blood flowed out of his face and his hands went cold.

"The other weakness Sal had, aside for a foolish trust in people, was drugs. He took the job loss hard. He took it personally. He had trusted the old woman, and she had betrayed him, threw him off for someone more pleasing to her."

"It was just a job," Danny said weakly.

"Oh, wonderful, then you shouldn't mind at all losing yours, or care in the least what happens to Margaret. She's just a woman who gave you … just a job."

Linus let it sink in a moment, sipping his coffee. "Sal was inconsolable. He was hurt and angry, not safe emotions for someone with addictions. He didn't believe he could take his anger out on Margaret, so he took it out on himself. Must I continue or do you remember him now?"

Danny waited, staring at Hern. "Yes," he said. "I remember him. I never knew what happened to him."

"Because you never cared," Linus hissed, sending shivers down the back of Danny's neck. "You never cared, that old woman never cared, nobody cared. He couldn't get clean again, Daniel, and six months later he was found in the Hudson River. It was not an accident. It was not some fun murder for your husband to solve. It was a sad, broken man ending his own life. And for that I vowed to someday destroy Margaret Bowman, her restaurant, and the man she threw Sal away for. Now if you'll excuse me - and even if you won't - I'll be leaving."

Linus slid out of the booth, watching Danny a final moment while Danny's gaze was frozen on the table. A ten dollar bill appeared in his line of sight as Hern threw it down. Danny looked up; he had never seen such hatred in a man's eyes before.

"I'm sorry," Danny said.

"Don't be. It's much too late. And don't think this is the end of it. Consider it a pause, now that you know what this has been about, this animosity between us all these years."

"No one ever told me."

Hern cut him off, leaning down into his space again. "Because it's none of their fucking business," he said slowly. "This is not for some sad gossip page. This is personal, private. And I'll be back. She'll have to sell to someone, and whoever it is will regret the day they got in my way. People who do that don't usually survive."

Danny knew he meant it, and that Linus Hern, now that his reasons were out in the open, would be more dangerous than ever.

"Give Kyle my congratulations on the photo exhibit," Linus said, turning to leave. "And my regrets. I'm previously engaged. I'll have to read the scathing reviews in the New York Times. Don't worry, their critic will be there, I made sure of that."

Linus Hern left him then, striding out of the restaurant with a spring in his step. The air had been cleared between them, but to Danny it felt like the preparing of a battlefield. The clouds had parted, the sun had come out, and beneath them the artillery was now in place. The first shot had been fired long ago; today the war had begun.

Danny motioned for the check. He wanted to be away from here as quickly as possible. Linus Hern had left a chill in his wake and Danny needed to be warm again.

Chapter Twenty-Seven

THE KATHERINE PRIDE GALLERY

The back office of the Katherine Pride Gallery had once been a utility closet. Kate had expanded it to twice the size, which made it just large enough for a small metal desk, two folding chairs and a water cooler that held a five-gallon jug. This was where many a hopeful artist first learned she would be stepping into the limelight with the blessing and support of one of Manhattan's most experienced art dealers. Kate Pride had been around long enough to be considered part of the establishment, but not long enough to be irrelevant. She knew the day was coming when she would be seen as entirely Old Guard and she didn't care. She loved sitting in this little office at her small gallery meeting new creative minds, welcoming new talent into the world.

"So," Linda said, sitting in the visitor's chair to the side of Kate's desk. "Here's what we're thinking."

"We? You have a partner?" Kate asked.

She glanced at her phone, noticing the red "message" light was on. Probably a call from her husband; they were set to have lunch again that afternoon.

Linda blushed at the question about a partner. She had several: Kirsten McLellan in New Hope, Bryan Frazier on the force, not technically a partner but the one other cop she'd really bonded with, and Kyle Callahan.

"Kyle," she said.

"Photographer Kyle?"

"Yes, that Kyle, the one who has a show here Friday night."

"He solves murders?"

Kate could tell Linda was becoming frustrated. "Sorry, I just had no idea. What is it you're thinking, you and Kyle?"

Linda reached for her tote bag, the one she'd bought at Grand Central with the subway map stenciled on it, and took out the New Year New Visions catalog. She placed it on the desk. "Someone involved, somehow, with the New Visions show is very unhappy and taking it out on the others." She looked gravely at Kate. "That could include you, Ms. Pride."

"Kate, please."

"Kate. After all, you're the ringmaster, if I may put it that way. I need to know what became of the others, the ones who aren't dead as far as we know, and especially the ones we'll never know at all."

Kate took the catalog and opened to the front. She remembered the artists very well. That year's New Visions show had been one of her most successful, in terms of launching the artists' careers. The show had become quite the hot ticket every January; style pages and art blogs across the city started anticipating the show as early as October, speculating on who might be included and what waves they would send through art circles.

"The graffiti couple are in Paris," Kate said. "I just read about them in Le Monde. That's the French paper. I don't speak it well but I can read fair enough. I'm a Francophile, what can I say. Suzanne DePris is in Seattle last I heard, and Javier Velasco's in Argentina."

"You know this for a fact? That they're all alive and well?"

"I don't know if they're well, that's a very broad term, but it's easy enough to find them and ask them."

"That's my next stop," Linda said. "Back to the hotel for research, then meeting Kyle at an event he went to. I'm very much in need of some answers by then. What about the ones you rejected?"

Kate closed the catalog and handed it back to Linda. "There weren't any," she said. "It doesn't work that way."

Linda put the catalog back in her bag. "How does it work then? I can't imagine you accept everyone who wants to be in the show."

"It's not a matter of acceptance or rejection. I find *them*, you see. Everybody knows about the New Year New Visions show, it's gotten a lot of attention, and people do try to persuade me, mostly agents and dealers. Some of the artists, sure. But my policy is also very well known. No one gets rejected because I do the asking. Submissions are not accepted. The New Year New Visions is an invitation-only show."

Invitation-only. No one gets rejected. The information didn't so much change things as narrow it. Detective Linda now knew she was looking at a smaller field, more limited choices. It had to be someone connected to the artists who had been in the show.

The thought hit her like ice water in the face. *What if it was one of the artists who* was *in the show?* What if success had not come to everyone – and why would it? Maybe one of them had found themselves in the shadows instead of the bright, warm light of fame? She needed to track them down, and quickly.

She thanked Kate for her time, feeling hurried now to narrow the field even more. The smaller the focus got, the closer they would be to an answer. As Kate Pride was showing her out, she stopped just in front of the desk. Corky quickly pretended to be looking at his computer, all the while listening for any scraps of data-power he could collect.

"Did any of them limp?" Linda asked.

"Limp?" said Kate.

Corky suddenly looked up.

"Yes, limp. Walk … differently."

"Oh my god," Corky said. "I tried to tell you! He was here. The guy with the limp."

Kate and Linda turned to him. Kate had no idea what the significance of the limping man was, while Linda knew very well and Corky, to his horror, guessed.

"You think he's the one doing this?" he said. "To Devin and Richard Morninglight? The man who was standing right where you are yesterday? Oh my god."

Kate remembered Kyle insisting someone had been watching them from across the street that Monday morning. Could it have been this man? And is he the one she remembered from the New Visions show, standing off to himself, peering at the opening night crowd from a corner?

"There was someone with a limp," Kate said, taking Linda gently by the arm and leading her away. Corky could be overly dramatic and she didn't want to fuel that fire. "But he wasn't one of the artists …"

Kate Pride walked out of the gallery with Linda, telling her what little she knew about the strange man. There wasn't much to tell, mostly whispers she had overheard.

She had no way of knowing he had heard them, too.

Chapter Twenty-Eight

HOTEL EXETER – CHECKOUT TIME

Kieran Stipling should have known better than to believe his troubled life had changed with the chance meeting of someone who claimed to see his inner beauty. He was a good looking man, that was true; he had always been attractive, handsome they said, and he had compensated for his misshapen hips by making sure that every other inch of him was superb. He'd begun working out as a kid, not yet a teenager, lifting and squatting and curling and pressing. By the time he was fourteen he had the physique of a young man who worked in a rock quarry or who had set his eyes on competition. He'd almost gone that route, too, into competition, where he would be able to show them all, but he had feared he would be seen as the exception, not the rule, the loser who managed to slip into a room of winners and deceive them just until his mask fell. Beneath the mask was a lonely child, molded more by his isolation and troubled emotions than he ever would be by his body. That was what Javier had told him, two years ago this coming June, and what he had believed until the truth came out. He had taken Javier's kisses for a guarantee they would always be together. He had opened the gates of his body and his heart, allowing this man in, this *other* whom he would have run from all his life before, and for his trust he had been betrayed. Abandoned. Turned out. Or so Javier thought. The amazing Javier Velasco. The shining new star that had shone so brightly even the lights of New York City could not obscure him. And once he knew it, once Javier Velasco saw himself the way all those fawning sycophants saw him, there was no room for something so flawed as his broken lover. Kieran and his crooked walk would draw the focus; people would whisper. Little had Javier known their whispers would be overheard and give rise to the shouts of Kieran's rage.

Katherine Pride and her wretched gallery were at the center of his pain. Until that show, until Javier had seen what could be his, had been told what could be his by that tight little circle of traitors, Kieran had believed they were inseparable. He had been happy in their studio apartment in Washington Heights, living among the Puerto Ricans, Dominicans, and the influx of the young with their big dreams in the big city. Kieran and Javier were just another couple in the neighborhood. The men who ran the corner bodega knew them. The old Korean woman at the Laundromat knew them. It had been a perfect life ... until that show. Until critics came around with their ten-dollar words and their blessings. Oh, how that had changed things. Javier Velasco was one to be watched. Javier Velasco was tomorrow's news. Javier Velasco was halfway up the mountain already, so talented, so gorgeous. Too bad he had that gimp tagging along. He could do so much better.

Javier believed them easily enough because he wanted to. He pretended nothing had change, for a month or two. They traveled. They went to San Francisco and Buenos Aires for Javier to be toasted by the town's art royalty; and the whispers had grown louder, the looks more cruel. Finally, Javier had said he had to go, Kieran with his sad eyes and his bad hips. He would always love Kieran, but they should be good friends, nothing more.

Nothing more.

The words echoed, bouncing off one side of Kieran's skull, careening to the other and back, as he stared up at the gray afternoon sky. *It's never really dark here*, he thought. Not the kind of dark you find on a country road.

Two things you cannot see in New York City: stars and the absolute, final, blackness of the universe. He intended to soon see them both. Once he was finished. He would take a bus and ride west, into the desert. Somewhere on the road to Las Vegas he would step off, never to be seen again. He would lie on his back and gaze up into an infinity wrapped in stars and blackness. And sometime, many years from now or maybe just a week, he would take his last breath attempting to count a billion flickering lights. Now it was afternoon and dreary, an appropriate landscape for the painting he had in mind.

Kieran felt a strange sadness as he prepared to leave the hotel room, the last place in New York City he would call home. It had been fitting: to go from living alone in a tiny basement apartment on the Lower East Side, to life with Javier in the upper reaches of Manhattan as their star – *their star* – was in its ascendency, to the unimaginable fall from grace that left him here in a hotel room that had seen a thousand like him. There were people who actually lived here, but most came and went like shadows moving across the filthy carpet. Some had left stains; he looked at one of them, a dark red oval near the closet, and wondered if it was blood. He would be gone in a moment, and the thousand who had come before him would be followed by a thousand after.

He packed his backpack with the few thing he would need: his one change of clothes, a toothbrush with no toothpaste, a pre-paid cell phone about to run out of minutes, his camera for capturing the finer moments just ahead, the ones that would make up his ultimate still life, and the knife he had used to kill Devin. He had exacted each revenge in a different way, with a different killer's tool. Only the knife would be a repeat performance. He had thought about trying to buy a gun, but he had no idea how one goes about purchasing a firearm on the streets of New York City. He'd bought cocaine once, from an itchy prostitute who walked the corner near his cousin's delicatessen in Flatbush, but that was the extent of his black market experience. He had quickly abandoned the idea of a gun and settled instead on the knife, a guitar string, and his own hands. He was his own weapon of choice, as it should be. He took full responsibility for what he was doing, and full pleasure in doing it. These people had harmed him irreparably; they had crushed his dreams as well as his soul. He had to settle accounts face to face, in as personal a way as possible.

Take it personally, Kate Pride. Take it very personally.

Today he would be closing out the accounts altogether. He had made an appointment to see a condominium in SoHo. The sort of living space he had visited recently as part of Javier's growing entourage, but that he would never, ever, live in. Those doors had been shut to him when he was turned away. But just this once, this one last time, he would stand in an apartment he could not dream of affording, smiling politely at Katherine Pride's husband – yes, yes, lovely closet space, the second bathroom is a bit small, but that view! – and waiting patiently for his wife to arrive. If it meant Stuart Pride took his last breath there, if things went a little wrong and there was collateral damage, so be it. That's what Kieran was, after all, collateral damage. But sometimes, yes, sometimes, the damaged strike back.

He zipped his backpack, slung it over his shoulder, and left the seedy little Hotel Exeter, knowing he would never return.

Chapter Twenty-Nine

THE KATHERINE PRIDE GALLERY

Corky was sipping blueberry herbal tea, watching Kate Pride show her husband the exhibit layout. The opening was Friday night and they had 125 registrations already. Fire code limited the number of occupants to 160 and Corky knew there would be a flurry of last minute comers. Shows at the Pride Gallery were a top ticket, not just to see the new artists being exhibited, but to be seen as well. Openings were about hobnobbing, glancing around for the nearest camera, complaining about the same papparazi they had tipped to their presence with a phone call on the way over. It didn't matter that no one had ever heard of the photographer Kyle Callahan. That was part of the experience, coming to see what new fabulous talent Kate Pride had discovered. Corky would be working the event and he looked forward to an evening of networking, moderate drinking of wine and eating of cheese, and possibly finding a new boyfriend. His last one, Phillip, had left a bitter taste in his heart and he was eager to move one. Nothing said 'next!' like a fresh romance.

Kate had shown Stuart the lineup of Kyle's photographs and he was duly impressed. He'd met Kyle and Danny a few times, and the couples had dinner once at Margaret's Passion, but they weren't more than acquaintances to him. Stuart and Kate Pride kept separate lives in many ways: professionally and, when they were not together, personally. Kate had her New York art world friends, her gallery, and her love of reading biographies; Stuart had his real estate sales, his preference for horror fiction, and his philately: Stuart was a stamp collector. Kate had no interest in stamps beyond how much it cost to do her gallery mailings.

The couple had enough common interests that being without children was of no significance to them. Of their parents, only Kate's mother remained alive, and her gay brother Douglas with his partner and three children provided all the extended family she needed. She could get her kid fix anytime by calling her young nephews and niece. Kate and Stuart had survived this long in a child-centric culture, they might as well go all the way.

Stuart looked at his watch. He'd had a new client call from out of the blue. The man had reached him directly, rather than going through his office. He thought it was odd at the time, since his cell number was private. When he asked the man how he got the number, the man told him Javier Velasco had given it to him. Stuart had shown the artist several one-bedrooms in TriBeCa just a month ago.

"Another showing?" Kate asked, seeing her husband look at the time.

"Yes, and it's a big one. Just came on the market. SoHo, three bedrooms, top floor."

"Anybody I know?"

Stuart smiled at his wife's curiosity. As the owner of a respected art gallery, Kate knew just about everyone there was to know in Manhattan's upper atmosphere, and if she didn't know them, she knew someone who did. Her Rolodex was her networking and in her opinion it still worked better than any social media. Index cards: the first LinkedIn.

"Possibly," he said. "A gentleman from Buenos Aries, says he got my number from Javier Velasco."

Corky looked up at the name. He thought of interrupting but decided it could wait. The Prides were a couple he hoped to emulate with his next boyfriend who would love him as completely and faithfully as Stuart loved Kate, and he didn't want to take a moment away from their time together. He knew their busy lives did enough of that.

"Ah, Javier, yes," Kate said. "Full of himself but talented. Sometimes I regret the egos I unleash on the world. He's in Buenos Aries now, from what I know."

"That's the connection then. Nouveau riche, I suspect."

"Oh, yes, of course. I've read a lot about that. Depressed housing market in the U.S., foreigners buying up all our best views. Be sure to invite him to the opening Friday. We take Argentine pesos, too."

They'd come back into the front of the gallery and were standing by the desk.

"I'll call you after this appointment," Stuart said. "Maybe we can have dinner."

"There's a new bistro on Gansevoort Street, Melissa's, I think it's called."

"Sounds fine to me, we like new places. Everything set for the opening here?"

She frowned. Mentioning the opening reminded her that the Katherine Pride Gallery was not MOMA. Everything here was done on a tight budget.

"I'd love to have passed hors d'oeuvres and hot waiters, or maybe it's passed waiters and hot hors d'oeuvres! But we don't have the funds and I want people looking at the photographs, not the men serving them Vienna sausages."

"You're a shrewd businesswoman, Kate Pride. Frugality is a virtue."

"It's about the art, not the money, right?"

"Right. We can leave the money making to me. Speaking of which, I have to dash."

Stuart Pride, standing a good five inches taller than the woman he had been in love with from the moment he'd met her, leaned down and kissed her, first on the cheek, and then, quite un-customarily in public – for Corky was considered public – he eased his face around and kissed her full-on on the lips. She, too, felt compelled to kiss him, long and deeply. It wasn't something they ever did when they could be seen, not in the gallery's front room, not on a street corner, and they were both taken by this sudden passion, this need.

Corky swiveled his chair around to face the wall, as if there were a spot on the paint he needed to inspect.

Finally, Kate and Stuart separated. She had blushed a bright red, and he kept looking down, embarrassed, but not apologetic.

"Well, that was unexpected," she said.

"Under the circumstances," he agreed, nodding toward Corky.

Kate ran her palms down the sides of her dress, as if they'd done more than kiss. "You'd better hurry," she said. "Cabs can be tricky here."

He kissed her once more on the cheek. "Call you," he said, and he left the gallery.

Kate watched after him. The passion of a moment ago was suddenly replaced by a longing sadness. It was as unexpected as their kiss had been, and she wondered where it came from. Was it age? Were they running out of time? She had the momentary, intense premonition that something terrible was coming their way. But those things were ridiculous, like imagining yourself falling from a subway platform when you never got that close to the edge. She felt strangely close to the edge. She shook it off, just as she'd shaken off the awkwardness of kissing her husband in front of Corky.

"You got a message," Corky said behind her. He'd turned back from the wall. "I didn't want to interrupt when you were talking."

She walked to the desk, expecting a message slip.

"Javier Velasco," Corky continued. "Another of your success stories. But he's not in Buenos Aires."

Kate was surprised to hear from Velasco. He'd quickly moved beyond the Katherine Pride Gallery, and while she didn't begrudge him his success, he was one of the few whose careers she wished she'd left for someone else to launch. Javier Velasco had the kind of self-regard that quickly went from down-and-out to entitled.

Corky saw her waiting for the message. "Oh," he said. "No number, nothing. He said he'd call back and was hoping to see you."

"Hmm," she said. Maybe he'd changed. Maybe some vicious critic in Argentina had taken him down a few pegs, or someone, somehow, had reminded him where he came from.

"Find me if he calls again, please," she said. "I'll be in the office." She wanted to go over the details of Friday's opening with Corky but would review them first, making sure she'd checked off everything she needed to do.

"Can I bring you anything?" Corky asked. "I'm dashing to Breadwinner's"

"I'm fine," she said. Then, as unexpectedly as she had kissed Stuart, she said, "Oh, and Corky, let's start locking this door, can we? I'll get a buzzer."

She looked around the gallery once more, picked up her iPad from the desk and headed to her office for some intimate time with a spreadsheet.

Chapter Thirty

BUENOS AIRES – TWO MONTHS EARLIER

T he Hotel Vista was located in the Puerto Madera Waterfront section of Buenos Aires. Situated on a significant slice of the Rio de la Plata riverbank, the area was home to some of the best and most current architecture the capital city had to offer. One of the newest neighborhoods in the city, it boasted theaters, restaurants, shopping for any taste, with an emphasis on the expensive. It was also home to the Hector Guiterrez Galeria del Arte, the top rung on the art ladder in all of the country, some said all of South America.

The Vista was a luxury hotel by definition: 120 rooms, a third of them suites, overlooking the river on one side and the vast city on the other. Attendants were at each guest's beck and call, and often showed up mysteriously and silently just when something was needed. There were two restaurants on the lobby floor, one that faced the street and catered to visitors to the area as well as hotel guests, and one tucked into the hotel with an entrance so discreet many people didn't realize it was there. That was where Javier Velasco had eaten his last meal with Hector Guiterrez on a

Wednesday night, expecting to attend the opening of his own show on Thursday. It was where he had enjoyed his fantasy of ever-greater fame and fortune, having moved quickly from the Katherine Pride Gallery to a show in San Francisco, and now this. It was like going from zero to sixty in five seconds, from selling paintings on the sidewalk outside the Metropolitan Museum of Art to having his work shown at the Modern. It was a rise that would have made most men's heads spin, but Javier Velasco was not most men, and he was certainly not most artists.

He had gone to dinner at 7:00 o'clock with the eminent Hector Guiterrez in the hotel's exclusive restaurant. Guiterrez had been attracted to Velasco's paintings from the moment he saw them in San Francisco. And, Kieran believed, the old man had been attracted to Javier as well. Kieran was no fool. He had not made it this far in life with a gimp's walk and the cruel whispers that followed it with contempt; he had not survived the brutality of children when he had been a child himself; he had not walked the gauntlet of a world bent on keeping him the butt of jokes, an object of ridicule, only to be run through by this "artist", this fraud. He had come to view Javier as a charlatan, a keen observer of what people consider important and great, and a manufacturer of those very things: art designed for the admiration of other artists, critics and gallery owners who could further his career. (Kieran had read once that poets wrote for other poets, which he decided may explain why nobody reads poetry.)

He should have known better than to think he was more than a distraction for Javier Velasco. Despite the hip dysplasia, he was in very good shape, and God had given him more than bragging rights in the dick department. It was amazing how many flaws men overlooked at the sight of a cock that made those flaws mere inconveniences. Velasco was no different. *Correction,* Kieran thought, sitting on the hotel bed, staring at the clock that now read nearly midnight: Velasco had professed his love, and Kieran Stipling had believed him. Stupidly. Blindly. Fatally for one of them.

His Greatness had made several critical mistakes. He had not wanted to be seen with his disabled lover, so he had arranged (with thin excuses to Kieran) to have them meet at the hotel rather than arrive together; nor would Kieran's name be on the registry. As far as the Hotel Vista was concerned, there was no Kieran Stipling, only a man they viewed later on security footage with his face obscured by a hoodie, and who limped as he walked to the room, then left in the middle of the night wheeling a large suitcase. Velasco had asked Kieran to go directly to the room. He had also neither introduced nor mentioned Kieran to anyone. It was as if Kieran Stipling did not exist. He certainly did not exist in the world in which Javier now moved. There was no room for imperfection in this world, and Kieran was quite imperfect. Except, as it turned out, when it came to evening the score: you treat me as a nonentity, I treat you as expendable; you treat me as an embarrassment, I leave you in a state of humiliation; you tell me you love me and then abandon me, I make sure you will never repeat that lie to anyone again.

Javier Velasco returned to the room just after 1:00 a.m. Kieran had been sitting on the bed for four hours. Javier wanted to go to bed, Kieran wanted to talk. More specifically, Kieran wanted to confront. What ensued was quick and brutal. Kieran Stipling knew his presence in the hotel was undetected and would only be discovered when they looked at the security tapes. That was why he had covered his face and kept it turned down. He had known what this would likely come to, and even though he had left room for a change in course, he hadn't expected it and it hadn't happened. What had happened was a fast, quick death. There could be very little argument, and no shouting. It would alert people. So Kieran had pressed his case very directly, accusing Javier of throwing him to the wolves now that he had moved into a world where wolves were plentiful and lambs like Kieran were free for the taking. He accused Velasco of preparing to dump him, to which an exasperated, egotistical and foolish Javier Velascao said yes, you're right, we're finished, now go.

Now go. Two words, served over ice. He was being dismissed, in a foreign country! Once it happened, as he had known it would, snapping Javier Velasco's neck had been, well ... a snap. Kieran had sighed and agreed to leave. He had come up behind Javier, who was taller by four inches, and put his arms around him for one last touch, a final embrace. And as Velasco started to pull away, Kieran Stipling pulled him back and down, snaking one arm around Javier's neck, and with his free hand quickly, ferociously, breaking his neck. It had been so easy, and so fast. Kieran hadn't expected it to be over that quickly. He was disappointed. But he was also in a hurry to be gone now. He emptied the large suitcase Velasco had brought with him and managed to just squeeze the artist's body into it. He hoped they would never find the suitcase with the corpse of the great Javier Velasco, but if they did, he would be long gone, back to New York City to deal with the people who had started it all, who had begun the whispers and brought about their own deaths.

Pulling the suitcase down the hall was awkward, and it kept nearly tipping over from the dead weight inside it. But Kieran was a strong man, and determined. An hour later he was on the southwest side of Buenos Aries in a massive and notorious landfill. He left his rental car parked near the landfill's edge and trudged, step by shaky step, into the landfill, where Javier Velasco would be attending the closing of his final show. No critics would rave, no buyers would bid. Only birds would come to pluck and rats to dine. The great artist would be climbing no more, and the cripple would go back into the shadows.

Chapter Thirty-One

THE CARLTON SUITES

Women in New York Media had been handing out their Women EmpOwering Women (WOW) Awards for the past twenty years. Imogene Landis had been to the luncheon ceremony a dozen times and had given up the idea that they were going to honor her with some kind of special award for effort. She hadn't even made the rather long short list in some time, so it was with humility, shock, and an I-said-I'd-be-back attitude that she went to the ceremony guaranteed a certificate. She knew half the women in the banquet hall of the Carlton Suites Hotel. They knew her, too, and as her career had driven slowly but inexorably into a ditch the last decade, they had begun to look away nervously when she came near. They would start to chatter about something inane, hoping that sad creature Imogene would hurry by and let them get back to real conversation. But not this time, oh no. This time she was number forty-seven out of fifty, and even though only the first ten were recognized from the stage, her name was in the program. Right there, between Sherri Vanguard, the pet reporter from Channel 7, and Elizabeth Darling, God rest her soul.

Kyle hadn't wanted to attend the event at all. He'd been there with Imogene two years ago and had seen how depressed and angry it made her to be treated like the has-been she was at the time. The murders at Pride Lodge had changed all that, and now she was a minor local celebrity at home and a cult favorite in post-midnight Tokyo. The looks they gave her today had been of envy, not pity. It was a lunchtime Imogene clearly enjoyed, but that Kyle had quietly, nervously, endured, while he kept checking his vibrating phone.

Detective Linda had been hard and fast on the job, tracking down the other artists from the New Visions show and she had information she kept feeding him as the luncheon dragged on. They were in the banquet hall for ninety minutes total, by the end of which Kyle was nearly ready to bolt. First had come a text from Linda that the graffiti artists were alive, well, and causing a stir in Paris as conjoined pop icons. Then came word that Suzanne DePris was living in Seattle and working as a florist. Apparently the art bug had bitten her, caused a minor irritation and moved on. And finally a startling text about Javier Velasco, the last of them to locate. "When RU finished?" she texted. "Big news on Velasco."

He had texted her back asking what the news was.

"Tell U in person," she wrote back. "On the way to hotel now."

Kyle looked at his watch. The last of the top ten recipients was at the podium carrying on much too long about her family and the job she would consider her most important forever and ever – that of mom to two precious sons, aged thirty-two and twenty-seven. He was about to lean over and tell Imogene that he had to leave, something urgent had come up, when applause broke out and for reasons he would never know the crowd stood to give the woman an ovation. She may have ended her speech with the announcement she was terminally ill, or given thanks to her stricken mother for setting an example. Something powerful that had them all standing and clapping, including Kyle, who mimicked the rest of them with no idea why.

"Thank God that's over," Imogene said, picking up her program as quickly as Kyle did before the applause had stopped. "They'll mail my certificate to me, let's get the hell out of here."

The two of them made a hasty exit, Imogene holding the hem of her dress up with one hand while she flagged a taxi with the other. One of a half dozen hovering near the hotel like vultures quickly pulled up to the curb.

"I'll be in later," Kyle said, opening the taxi door for Imogene. "I've got a few things to do."

"Of course you do," she said. "Your big opening's on Friday. I can't wait! You must be a nervous wreck. In fact, take the day. I'll see you in the morning."

As the taxi sped off, Kyle looked up and saw Linda walking quickly up the sidewalk toward him.

"They found him," she said, out of breath. She'd taken the subway and had dashed two blocks from the station to the hotel.

"Who?" Kyle asked, confused. "The killer?"

"No! Javier Velasco, the artist. They found him. Or what's left of him."

"Oh my God."

"I don't think God was anywhere in the vicinity when this happened."

She pulled him aside, letting the flow of exiting guests get past them to the curb. More taxis had miraculously arrived, swarming the front of the hotel.

"Some kids playing in a landfill found him, outside Buenos Aires."

Kyle's face fell. He knew what was coming next.

"We're dealing with a very dangerous man here," she said, "Javier Velasco's body was stuffed inside a suitcase. It hit the Argentine news over the weekend."

"I'm surprised we didn't hear about it here."

"That's because they didn't know whose body it was! It was only identified yesterday. And if he's as big a name in the art world as you say ..."

"About to be."

"About to be ... then we'll see something tonight, tomorrow at the latest. Javier Velasco is dead, and not by natural causes."

Kyle's head was spinning. The connections had been made and were pointing in only one direction.

"There's more," Linda said. "Kate Pride knew the limping man. Not well, she didn't even speak to him, but he was at the New Visions show."

"I looked at the photos ..."

"You can't see a limp in a photograph, Kyle."

She was right, of course. He'd been looking for a man he only vaguely recognized from across the street, and only glimpsed for an instant. "So who is he?"

"Javier Velasco's partner. Boyfriend. Lover. All of the above."

"Clearly now an ex. I don't think they'll be getting back together." He took her by the arm and started walking west. "We have to see Kate, immediately."

"Where are we going?" Linda said, glancing back at the dozen taxis and two dozen people trying to get them.

"Seventh Avenue, we'll get a cab faster there. These people coming out of the hotel are ruthless."

The two of them fast-walked along 56th Street, cars passing them in the opposite direction as Kyle hurried toward Seventh. Time was escaping them and none could be spared. If the killer had started with Javier Velsaco, and Richard Morninglight was his most recent kill, he was getting very close, his death spiral tightening. Kate had to be warned ... or saved.

They crossed the sidewalk at Seventh Avenue and Kyle led them into the street, raising his hand frantically. A taxi pulled to the curb and the two of them got in, leaving an irate woman with a suitcase on wheels shrieking at them for stealing her cab. Oh well, Kyle thought, that's Manhattan. You win some, you lose more. He ignored the woman's cries as they veered into traffic heading downtown.

Chapter Thirty-Two

Twelve Floors Above SoHo

Few sights of urban life are more breathtaking than the New York City skyline, among the most recognizable in the world. It had changed, admittedly, since the loss of the massive Twin Towers on 9/11, once magnificent bookends to the city's panorama, but it remained a breathtaking vision, whether seen from across the river in Brooklyn or Queens, from a taxi driving in from an airport, or from twelve stories up in an apartment overlooking downtown Manhattan. That was the view Stuart Pride was showing off now, to a stranger who had yet to give him any real information about himself, except to say he'd gotten Stuart's private number from an artist they both knew.

Stuart Pride was not superstitious or easily spooked, but something about the man made the hair on his arms stand up; it was an undefined chill, and he wrote it off to the building's heat being low or the cool April air.

The apartment was spectacular, there was no doubting that, and Stuart was counting on its sale to provide his best commission of the year. New York City, Manhattan specifically, had not suffered nearly as much during the nation's ruinous housing bust as the rest of the country. And while many Americans were priced out of a stubbornly high market, there were plenty of foreigners who saw property here as a steal and a sound investment. There would be no foreclosure crisis in the nation's biggest city, except for the unfortunate ones who lost their jobs and should probably never have moved here in the first place.

They were currently twelve floors above Prince Street, in one of Manhattan's most famous neighborhoods, SoHo. Shorthand for "SOth of HOuston," the area had for decades been a home to art galleries and the trendiest of the trendy, and while it now had competition from areas like the Meatpacking District and galleries like Katherine Pride's, it remained a popular tourist destination and among the most expensive places in the city to live. The apartment Stuart was currently showing had three bedrooms, two and a half baths, a kitchen the size of most studio apartments, and a spectacular terrace overlooking downtown Manhattan. The asking price was a cool $2.5 million, a steal by anyone's reckoning. Something about the client made Stuart wonder if he really had that kind of money. He had already cursed himself for not directing the man to his office where he could be properly screened. The thought of selling his most expensive apartment of the year had clouded his judgment; greed had gotten the best of him, and he made a mental note not to let it happen again.

"What is it you do again, Mr. Stipling?" Stuart asked. He seldom showed apartments to people carrying backpacks, and only when the occasional rock star came his way did they look so much like they would never see two million dollars in their lives. Make that two and a half million.

"Art," Kieran said. He had been standing by the glass doors that opened out onto the terrace, looking up and around, as if he wanted to see how exposed it was to the views of neighbors.

"Ah, yes, art. My wife's in the art business, but you must know that through Mr. Velasco. Kate doesn't really see it as a business. She has the heart of an altruist. What part of the art world do you specialize in, may I ask?"

"Call me an accountant."

Stuart thought it was a strange way to phrase it.

Kieran saw the look on his face and smiled ever so slightly. "I settle accounts, let's put it that way."

"For Javier Velasco?"

"He was one of them, yes."

Was one of them, past tense. Another odd choice of words. Stuart had become very apprehensive and wanted to get the showing over as soon as possible. The spacious apartment with the amazing views was suddenly stifling.

"Let's take a look at the gym," Stuart said. "The building offers quite an impressive one on the second floor. It's free to tenants, of course."

"I'd like to see the terrace," Kieran said, as if he hadn't heard him. Without waiting for a reply, he opened the sliding door and stepped out. He glanced quickly up and around, noticing that no buildings overlooked them: they were effectively hidden from view in a city of eight million people. It was too early for plants, but there were several large planters along the edge, where a black wrought-iron gate encircled the space. In the corner, overlooking Broadway, was a glass table with four chairs, all black iron to match the gate. A large umbrella that would fit into the table's center lay on its side, waiting for warmer weather.

Stuart followed Kieran out. He'd never liked heights and stayed away from ledges, but he had a client to please, and the sooner that was done, the sooner they could leave.

"Oh, look!" Kieran said, leaning slightly over the railing and looking down. "You won't see that anywhere but New York City."

As Stuart crossed the terrace to where he was standing looking down, Kieran's hand slipped unnoticed into his backpack.

Stuart stepped up next to him, leaned carefully over the gate, just enough to see the sidewalk twelve floors below. There was nothing of note to be seen. He was about to ask what Kieran had been looking at when then the thin rope slipped around his neck, looping quickly again in his first startled moments. Kieran pulled him back with it, as if it were a leash or the reins on a horse. Stuart stumbled and fell face down on the terrace floor, gashing his nose. Blood began to flow from a nostril and his eyes watered from the impact. He grabbed blindly at the rope around his neck, desperate to loosen it.

"Don't worry," Kieran said, pushing Stuart back down with a foot on his back. "I'm not going to kill you. Not yet."

Stuart struggled to get up, one hand on the stone terrace trying to push himself up, the other grasping for the iron fence.

Kieran shoved him back down. He reached into Stuart's pocket and dug around until he found his cell phone.

"I'm going to strangle you now," Kieran said. "But don't worry. It's only enough to make you pass out. When you come to again you'll be manageable. These chairs look very uncomfortable, but sturdy. In the meantime, I have a text message to send. What was your wife's number? Oh wait, it's on speed dial. I bet she comes when you call her." Kieran laughed at his own crude joke and began searching for Kate Pride's name in the contact list. "Imagine her surprise when you tell her Javier's here."

Stuart Pride thought desperately of a way out, a means of escape, but his thoughts were cut short as Kieran knelt beside him and tightened the rope. His air gone, his head feeling as if it would explode, Stuart Pride gave himself to the blackness.

Chapter Thirty-Three

THE KATHERINE PRIDE GALLERY

Corky was sitting behind the front desk when Kyle and Linda hurried into the gallery. It was nearly two o'clock and there was only one person there, a woman looking intently at one of the collages in the open showroom as if she were meditating upon it. Customers were sparse even on a busy day, it was just the nature of the beast. The survival of a gallery like Kate Pride's depended on a slow but steady stream of sales, not volume, and certainly not discounts. People who bought the artists on exhibit here were getting the best discount they could hope for, although it came with a gamble: someday, the sooner the better, the artists whose work they purchased would be further up the fame ladder, going from unknown to heard-of to must-have, at which point the painting or the photograph they bought for $1500 would be worth many times that. It didn't always work that way and there were just as many artists whose art depreciated as there were whose works tripled in value, but that's the way it went. No risk, no gain, and Kate Pride had founded her gallery on risk.

Corky looked up, surprised to see Kyle and the lady cop. He put his copy of Architectural Digest on the counter. Fantasizing living in homes he would never set foot in was one of his favorite time killers.

"Is Kate here?" Kyle asked, clearly agitated.

"No, she went out. Isn't it bad luck or something for you to be here before the opening?"

"That's weddings, or something, and no, it's not bad luck. Do you know where she went?"

"She'll be back in an hour," Corky said. One of his boss's rules was to never tell anyone where she was, unless she had an appointment with them. She thought the world had become entirely too invasive, with smartphones tracking you everywhere and Google Maps vans driving around videotaping every street corner. It gave her the creeps, and she didn't want anyone knowing her whereabouts who she hadn't told herself.

"This is important, Corky," Kyle said. He had not made any attempt over the previous weeks to befriend the young man and now regretted it.

"I'm sure it is, but ..."

"It's a police matter," Linda interrupted. She'd noticed earlier the deference Corky paid to authority. "We think she's being followed and there's really no time to waste."

"Let me call her."

"I've been doing that for the last fifteen minutes, Corky." Kyle tried his hardest not to let his irritation show. "She's not answering."

By then Corky had already grabbed his desk phone and dialed Kate's cell number. He held a finger up to tell them to wait just a moment; Kyle imagined bending it backward and breaking it. Corky frowned and held the receiver away from his ear, letting them hear the sound of Kate's recorded voice asking the caller to leave a message.

"She's with Stuart, her husband," Corky said, slapping the phone down. "How much safer could she be?"

Kyle and Linda looked at each other. If she was with Stuart, all should be fine, at least for now. It would buy them precious time.

"He's showing an apartment to one of Javier Velasco's friends."

Kyle stopped cold. "Javier Velasco?"

"Yes. He's in town. She got a text from Stuart just awhile ago, this Velasco guy met them at the condo and Stuart asked her to come by. He probably thinks it will seal the deal, he's all about selling his apartments."

"Where is this condo?" Kyle asked.

"I don't know. She didn't give me an address."

"Call his office and find out," Kyle said. "Please, Corky. Now."

Corky picked the phone up and began to dial Stuart Pride's real estate office.

Linda leaned in, impressing on Corky the urgency of the moment. "And once we have the address, we need you to call the police and have them meet us there."

"Does this have something to do with ..." Corky said, his voice trailing off. "Oh my God."

His hands were shaking as he grabbed a notepad and pen, waiting for an answer at the realtor's office.

"Janet?" he said. "This is Corky at the gallery, I need to know where Stuart is. The condo he's showing. I know it's not on his calendar! Just give me the address, please, this is official police business."

Kyle turned to Linda. "Get us a taxi. Tell him I'll be right out."

Linda hurried out of the gallery as Corky began to write furiously. As soon as the address and apartment number were on the notepad, Kyle reached over, grabbed the top sheet and ran for the door.

Chapter Thirty-Four

TWELVE FLOORS ABOVE SOHO

K ate Pride had lived in New York City for twenty-five years and never feared for her life until this moment. Manhattan had remained for her a place of dreams, the Emerald City far in the distance, but not so far she couldn't get there if she tried hard enough and believed in her own potential. Some would call her life charmed; she had not, upon reflection, experienced much difficulty here, no real obstacles to her ambitions. She'd set the trajectory for her life early and mostly just held on for the ride, picking up Stuart along the way, her years learning from the best in the business, her gallery that had never really struggled, and here it all was coming to a sudden and terrifying end.

Stuart was secured to his chair on the terrace with duct tape Kieran had bought on the way from the Hotel Exeter. Along with a spindle of clothes line rope, the purchase had left him with $75 and change to his name; even a bus wouldn't get him far for that, but he had stopped worrying much about his future plans when he left Javier Velsaco's body in an Argentine landfill. Kieran, too, had led a charmed life, at least the last two months of it. The killings had been easy; he'd not taken great precautions, just covered his face and kept his presence unknown to most but his victims, yet here he was, twelve floors above SoHo, on a terrace with a spectacular view that could not be viewed – in New York City, of all places! – and no authorities were coming. No police hot on his trail. He was as much a phantom as a man can be, come back to haunt the ones who whispered. Call it lucky, call it charmed, everything had finally gone his way, and he felt great.

Kate had arrived thinking she was meeting Stuart, Javier and a friend of his looking to buy an expensive apartment. Roscoe the doorman had let her pass without even calling up. Stuart was one of three real estate agents authorized to sell in the building, and Roscoe had seen him come and go dozens of times; there was no reason to bother using the intercom, so he let Kate breeze by and take the elevator to the twelfth floor. He was calmly going through deliveries from the dry cleaners, logging them into the building's online system, while Kate was being bound to a chair next to her husband.

When she got to the apartment the door was open a crack, and Kate should have hesitated then. Stuart was meticulous about these things and never left apartment doors open, even in buildings as secure as this one. She knocked and called out. "Stuart? Are you there?" At first there was no response, and she checked her text message to make sure she had the right address. Stuart brokered a half dozen buildings in this area, there could be a mix up.

"We're on the terrace," a strange man's voice said. It was her second missed opportunity to back away. Why would a stranger answer when she called out her Stuart's name?

Remaining outside in the hall, she said, "Is Stuart there? Am I at the right apartment?"

Kieran opened the door, startling her. "Yes, yes, you must be Kate Pride. Stuart and Javier are on the terrace, it's an amazing view. Come in, please."

Kate still felt something was off, but the man seemed nice enough, and his voice was gentle, his smile sincere. There was also something familiar about him. She entered the apartment, distracted by the sheer size and comfort of it. Just as Kieran closed the door behind her, she remembered with a sudden shock where she'd met him and who he was. She had tried to describe him just an hour ago to that woman detective, tugging at her memories to remember what he looked like. And now she knew.

By then Kieran had placed himself between Kate and any hope of escape.

"How do you not fear for your life riding taxis in this city?"

Linda was completely sincere in her question. This was the third time in two days she had ridden in a cab and each time had been a thrill of the worst kind. "Please put your seatbelt on," she added. "I haven't known you long enough to lose you to a traffic accident."

Kyle was leaning up against the partition, staring at the street ahead as if he could magically make them go faster. The taxi was already speeding, veering from lane to lane as it barreled toward SoHo. Kyle had offered the driver an extra $20 to get them there in ten minutes.

"Relax," he said. "New York City streets are among the safest in the world. Very few people die in traffic here."

Linda found that hard to believe. She'd observed since arriving that walk lights had no meaning here. People swarmed along this way and that, paying no mind whatsoever to traffic lights. It seemed like orchestrated chaos, with cars hurtling through lights and pedestrians walking between them, somehow gauging the distance available and the time it would take them to cross in front of the cars without being hit. It was almost mystical, but unnerving, and she wanted no part of it. She had dutifully waited for a 'walk' light at every corner she'd been on. As for taxis, the sooner she was out of this one the better, and she planned to familiarize herself with the subway system and buses on any future visits.

Kyle had called and texted Kate twice to no avail since they got into the cab. He had also called Corky to make sure he'd notified the police. Corky assured him they were on the way, but that he'd had a hard time explaining the emergency to them. "Someone could get killed" struck the 911 dispatcher as vague and overly dramatic. Corky spent five minute convincing her it wasn't a prank. The best the dispatcher would do is promise him she would send a cruiser to check it out.

"Here!" Kyle shouted. "First building on the left, that's it."

The taxi swerved to the curb, nearly hitting an elderly woman walking an equally elderly Jack Russell Terrier. Once again Linda was awed by the symphony of anarchy, as the old woman didn't so much as glance at the cab that nearly took her life. She tugged on the dog's leash and walked down the sidewalk.

Kyle grabbed two twenties from his wallet and handed them to the driver, a man of Middle Eastern descent and demeanor who had whispered illegally into a headset all the time he was driving. No acknowledgment had been made of his passengers other than to agree to the extra $20. He had gotten them to their destination with a minute to spare.

Linda and Kyle hurried into the building. Roscoe stepped from behind the front desk to stop them when he saw them rushing in. "Excuse me, are you here to see someone?"

"Kate Pride," Kyle said. "She's here with her husband, showing an apartment."

"I'll have to call up," Roscoe said.

"There's no time."

"I can't let you go. Just a moment, please."

Roscoe walked back behind the desk and picked up the phone. Kyle and Linda could hear it ringing as Roscoe held it out from his ear. "That's odd, there's no answer."

"Please," Kyle said. "There's no time."

"Maybe they're on the terrace," Roscoe continued. "I can try calling back in a few minutes."

Linda pulled out her New Hope detective's badge for the second time. "This is a police matter, we really don't have time."

Roscoe nodded, of course, please, go right ahead.

"We need the keys," Kyle said, knowing every doorman kept keys to the empty apartments. Roscoe hesitated again. It was in his training to be cautious, to not assume anything was as it seemed. The city was too full of scammers and con artists, you had to be vigilant.

"Now!" Linda shouted, shocking the doorman into action. He could lose his job for this, or be a hero. He said a quick prayer and fumbled in the closet for the keys to 12D.

Kate had never imagined her life ending on the terrace of an apartment in SoHo, in full view of anyone who had been able to see them, but no one was. The terrace was on the top floor facing south, and no other building overlooked it, nor were any close enough for people in the windows to see without using binoculars. It was the perfect terrace to kill someone on, and Kieran thanked Stuart for providing such an outstanding location. Stuart only looked at him in terror, his mouth sealed with the same duct tape that bound his hands and feet to the chair. His wife, the love and center of his life, was equally helpless, confined to a chair just a few feet from him. They could only stare at each other, attempting to communicate with their eyes as they wavered between fear and hope, determination to survive and unspeakable grief at the certainty they would not.

Kyle snapped another photograph of the couple with his camera. He'd been waiting to use it, and regretted not thinking to buy it before. He would have loved to make a slideshow of photos from the hotel rooms in Buenos Aires and Philadelphia, the landfill and the rain-soaked sidewalk in Brooklyn. Oh well, he told himself, you can't have everything.

"I know you were one of the whisperers," Kieran said to Kate, leaning in and snapping a close up of her terrified face as she shook her head, denying any part in his crazed ideas. "I even think you started it."

She shook her again. She knew the man was insane, and she knew he was capable of killing because he already had. She needed to convince him of her innocence.

"Oh, yes, Katherine, you're the queen bee, it's your gallery. I saw you. You and Javier, Richard Morninglight, Devin and that Shiree woman. Talking and whispering, laughing and whispering. I watched you closing night at the restaurant celebrating. I wasn't invited. Did you know that?"

She remembered then: a congratulatory dinner with the people he'd named. The other artists didn't join them. It wasn't planned, just an impromptu meal at Trattoria Del Amo. They'd walked there the night of the New Visions closing to celebrate their success and toast their futures.

Kieran saw that Kate remembered, and he smiled. "Now it comes back. You and the others. Talking about your triumph. Telling Javier he would be better off without me. I was a stone around his neck. What's the word?

'Albatross.' What a strange thing to wear around your neck, a dead bird. I don't want any albatrosses around my neck, but I'm happy to be one around yours. And I am sorry your husband has to pay this price. At least you'll be on camera together." He showed her the small camera he'd spent too many precious dollars on. "It takes video, too. I'm going to be the next YouTube sensation. Well, you are, anyway. It may be the first snuff film to make the morning news. How's that for high art?"

Kate's mind was turning round and round. She began to twist her wrists, knowing it was futile but hoping to somehow break free. She looked across at Stuart and saw he was doing the same, and had begun to buck in the chair as if he might be able to leap up still fastened to it but furious enough to free them while they still had time.

Kyle and Linda burst from the elevator into the 12th floor hallway.

"Every front desk has a set of keys," Kyle said, explaining why Roscoe had them. "For most of the apartments, tenants like knowing someone can get in if they have to. And definitely the ones for sale. He has to let the brokers in."

Linda didn't care why they had the keys, only that they did. They rushed to apartment 12D.

Kieran heard them fumbling with the lock, then bursting into the apartment. It was both a surprise, and expected. He had fantasized the final kill, the tableau he'd set over and over in his mind that would play out on computers and televisions around the world, yet he had wondered with each successive murder why he had not been caught. At first he had truly believed he had the power of invisibility, but then he thought he was just very lucky, that God was on his side, the side of right. And yet, he knew the time may come, he may find himself in exactly this situation, having raced so far but unable to make it the last few yards to the finish line.

With no time to think it through, no moment to wonder who was rushing toward the terrace, Kieran stepped around behind Kate Pride and placed his knife at her throat, the same knife he had used to stab Devin sixteen times.

Linda and Kyle ran onto the terrace – and froze.

"Ah," Kieran said, holding Kate's head back with one hand, the knife with the other. "The photographer. I recognize you. I watched you from the coffee shop across the street. No camera today? It's okay, you can have mine."

Kyle wanted to reason with an unreasoning man. Knowing it was about buying time and not doing something that would get Kate Pride's throat cut, he said, "I didn't realize who you were."

Kieran stared at him, his expression growing darker. "You still don't," he said. "No one realized who I was until it was too late. Javier certainly didn't know who I was. He thought I was just another throwaway. And the fuckers who told him that made him sure of it, including the woman you're about to watch die."

"Kate never said anything about you. I was there." Kyle recognized him now from some of the photos he'd taken at the New Visions opening. "You were against the wall. No one understood how important you were."

"You're not serious," Kieran said. "You think this is a movie? You think you can just flatter me or pretend you have the slightest idea who I am and I'll, what, give you the knife? Surrender? Let's hear what Kate thinks about that. I'm going to take the tape off her mouth, and if she so much as breathes too deeply, I'm going to kill her."

Kieran reached down with his free hand and yanked the tape from Kate's mouth. "Tell them," he said.

She tried not to gasp for air, worried it would set him off. "Tell them what?" she managed.

"The same things you told Javier, the same things all of you told him, why he tossed me away like a tissue he'd just cum on, why I left his body in a landfill."

The sirens could be heard then, closing the distance to the building. Kieran cocked his head, listening. Sirens were a common sound in Manhattan, but he knew these were for him.

When Kieran turned his head to listen for the approaching sirens, Linda began to ease down ever so slightly, at the same time lifting her right leg, reaching very carefully for her ankle holster. She had never told Kyle she carried a gun off duty; there was no reason to, but she'd been around guns her entire life. She has seen her father's police service pistol, and many like the one that killed him in front of that Cincinnati grocery store. She cursed herself for not taking it out sooner, but the time for regret was over. She could think it through later, if they all made it out alive.

"I told Javier he was lucky to have you," Kate said. "No one wants to be alone in the world. Javier wanted someone to share his success with, that someone was you."

"You don't even know my name," Kieran hissed. "And you're a very bad liar. You all whispered to him, then you laughed and toasted your own cruelty. I saw you, just like I saw you yesterday. I've been watching you, Katherine Pride, watching and waiting."

The sirens had grown louder, screaming down the street until they stopped in front of the building. It was only a matter of moments now.

Stuart Pride had been watching it all, trying to calm himself. He saw Linda begin to ease down. The two of them exchanged glances as she shook her head almost imperceptibly, telling him not to do anything stupid. He understood what she was doing and nodded, knowing he would ignore her anyway. The window of opportunity had opened just a crack and he had to act before it closed forever. Linda had her hand nearly to her ankle, and with just a minor distraction she would be able to reach it. He took a quick breath through his nose and flung himself to the side, crashing to the terrace floor and smashing his head on the tiles.

Kieran jumped back, and at that very moment Linda squatted down and slid her gun out from its holster. Faster than the eye could see, quicker than the mind could calculate, she had the gun raised and aimed squarely at Kieran Stipling's chest.

"Drop the knife," she said. "I'm a cop, I know how to shoot and I won't hesitate."

Kieran raised his hands, the knife still in his right fist, but he made no move to surrender.

"Do you know my name?" Kieran asked, as he began to step slowly backward.

"Stop," Linda said, knowing what he was thinking.

"Who am I, cop lady? Call me by name."

"You're a man who needs understanding," Linda said. She began to ease toward him, holding her free hand out. "Just give me the knife. We can get help for you."

"You don't even know my fucking name!" Kieran shouted, the rage in his voice echoing off the terrace floor, the apartment door, the rooftops around them, out, out into the sky. A cry of pain and anguish unlike anything any of them had ever heard.

It all happened so fast that afterward each of them told a slightly different version. A neutral observer would say that Kieran, knowing his time had come and there was no way out, no bus he would ever be catching to a back road somewhere to disappear, flung the knife at Linda, catching her off guard just long enough to sidestep to the terrace railing.

"Don't do this," Linda said in a last effort to stop him.

"What are my alternatives?" Kieran replied.   He was strangely calm. It was the demeanor of a man who knew he had no options. But Kieran Stipling had always known that. His life was one of decisions made to survive, not to prosper, not to create a life that was anyone's dream come true, least of all his. He had been thrown about by circumstances, and had only once believed things had gone his way. Once, with a man named Javier Velasco, who proved to be as cruel as the rest of them.

So fast. No negotiation, no possibilities. It was breathtaking, how suddenly and easily he went over the railing. Unbelievably fast and easy, so easy that Linda and Kyle kept staring at the space where Kieran had just been. Kate and Stuart Pride couldn't see what happened, and stared up dumbfounded at the shock on their faces. It took Linda several seconds before she ran to the railing, leaning out and looking down.

Roscoe the doorman was already standing over the body. A young couple had nearly been hit by Kieran as he landed on the sidewalk, and the woman began to scream.

Chapter Thirty-Five

OPENING NIGHT

More had happened in one week than in any week of Kyle's life he could remember. Just six days ago his first love had gotten married, bringing Kyle both happiness for David, and sadness at such a clear sign of time passing. They had barely been men when they moved to New York City, and now, thirty-five years later, David had married, Kyle and Danny were in the planning stages of their own wedding, and youth for all of them was the stuff of reminiscence.

Then came the news reports of Devin's murder, the arrival of Detective Linda, and the spiral of events that ended so horribly on a terrace in SoHo – and a sidewalk twelve stories below. Even the murders at Pride Lodge had not been such a jolt. And while all of it unfolded, this was always in the background waiting to happen, his opening night. It had gone on as planned, everyone was here, and yet it all felt surreal to Kyle as he sipped a glass of wine and listened to another compliment from another stranger on his beautiful photographs.

Kyle had been making his photos public for over a year on a Tumblr photoblog. The idea of people seeing his pictures was nothing new. But this was different, this was *official*, not quite professional, but very close to it. Professionals were born of gallery shows like this. Word would spread, but luckily for Kyle he was not a portraitist. He would not be taking calls from people looking for someone to shoot their wedding or their black tie event at the Met. His was a photography of isolation, pictures that featured angles, various forms of natural light, *vision*scapes as much as landscapes. The word approached his lips but he held it back, having been afraid to think it, let alone say it ... *art*. Did he dare call it that? He'd considered himself a shutterbug, nothing more. But to be an *artist*? He was uncomfortable with the term, as afraid to be pretentious as he was to be wrong.

He looked around the gallery. Margaret sat in a one of several chairs that had been provided, holding court with a handful of people. She seemed to know more guests among the crowd than nearly anyone else but Kate Pride herself. Nearly 200 people had shown up, only about a dozen of whom Kyle could address by name. Had it been wrong of them to still have the opening after everything that happened? Kieran Stipling's suicide had been two days ago; it was still news, and Imogene Landis had already begun spinning it into her next big scoop. Kyle had promised her that, and no sooner had he and Danny given statements at the police station, than Imogene began calling to remind him of her exclusivity. Such was the stuff of love-hate relationships. It was horrific, yet seedy; tragic, yet someone must tell the story. Why not Imogene Landis? For all her faults, Kyle loved her.

His mother was another woman he loved, but whose faults were harder to name. Sally Callahan had arrived that afternoon, and rather than tell Kyle and Danny her big secret, she had brought him with her: Farley Carmichael, the man she had been seeing for two months without saying a word about it. No doubt she had wanted to wait until she was sure of her feelings, but it had come as a shock to Kyle. His mother was seventy-six years old and had sworn she would never love any man but Bert Callahan. Showing up with a boyfriend almost ten years younger and beaming non-stop since she arrived was not something Kyle had ever anticipated or even entertained. It wasn't that he thought his mother was betraying his late father, that would be ridiculous. But Sally had been so sure she would live out her years as a single widow. His discomfort with it was only heightened when she told him she and Farley would be staying at the Westin. One room, one bed.

"They look great together," Danny said, startling Kyle out of his thoughts. "And what better time to offer her ownership in a restaurant than now, when her life is so new?"

"Of course she'll say yes," Kyle said. "Be very careful what you wish for in this case, Daniel. She won't be the silent partner you're imagining."

Kyle only called him Daniel when he was being extra serious. Danny knew they'd be continuing this conversation for years to come and he didn't care right now. His beloved Margaret and her equally beloved restaurant would be safe. "Timing is everything," he said, as much to himself as to Kyle.

"Appearances, too," replied Kyle, quoting his boss. "They certainly appear happy."

Sally and Farley were across the room, admiring Kyle's "Lonely Blue Pool" photo. It seemed to catch everyone's attention and he was beginning to think he could sell prints of it. Soon it might show up in every bargain-rate hotel room in the country and Kyle would be set for life.

"Why the secrecy?" Kyle asked. They had both liked Farley well enough on first inspection. Sixty-seven, tall, handsome with pure silver hair, still thick and brushed back; sensible half-frame gold glasses, the hands of a piano player, with long thin fingers, a gray moustache, and a very good dresser who knew how to be formal and casual at the same time. Farley Carmichael was retired, but comfortably so. He'd sold yachts for a living, and clearly made a profit. And then there was the adoration in his eyes as he stayed close to Sally. So affable, so likeable, so perfect for her. Something must be wrong.

"She knew it would be hard for you," Danny said, sipping his Vodka martini. "Your relationship with your dad was a tough one, but he was still your dad. There's a reason you wanted that desk."

Kyle let it go. He'd told himself the desk was a keepsake, but he knew Danny was right. He knew it was more complicated than simply wanting a memento. And he knew his mother's happiness was most important. Whatever misgivings he had, he would deal with later. Even if it meant more time on a therapist's couch.

Kate Pride was working the crowd, truly a professional. Stuart had been too shaken by the events of the past three days and had bowed out. He'd taken time off from work as well and once the opening was over he and Kate were planning an unexpected trip to Paris. It was their favorite city, and Stuart, realizing how precious time is and how suddenly life can take a tragic turn, wanted them to go there again. It had been ten years since their last trip, and every spring they promised to visit, only to have it postponed for one thing or another. No more postponements, Stuart told her that morning. No more waiting for next year to do the things that matter.

Nothing new had been learned about Kieran Stipling since he plunged to his death from the SoHo terrace. It turned out the view wasn't as hidden as he'd thought, and several frantic calls had been placed to 911 from people in distant buildings watching something frightening unfold twelve floors above Manhattan. He was an enigma, this damaged man projecting his suffering onto his victims, blaming them for a life he hated. The trail he left was a jagged one, crisscrossing the country over the course of twenty years, and it would be several months before a clearer picture of him emerged. Now, in the immediate aftermath, he remained a mystery, with a past as opaque as a fog rolling in off the Hudson. A man who had come from the shadows and quickly, instantly, returned to them. An invisible man whose existence was only proved by his body on the sidewalk.

Kyle felt a tap on his shoulder and turned to see who it was. He didn't know Detective Linda had any friends in New York City, and for a moment he wondered where she had been hiding this one as Linda started to introduce him to a woman nearly as tall as she was. Then it hit him before she even spoke: he was looking into the smiling face of Kirsten McClellan.

"Kyle and Danny, meet Kirsten," Linda said. "Kirsten, this is Kyle and Danny."

She was a looker, Kyle saw that immediately. Short brown hair with just hints of gray, lithe in her posture, like a cheetah, he thought, slim and dressed to kill in a navy pantsuit that had to have cost as much as most people paid for a month's rent.

"I had to come," Kirsten said. "After everything that happened."

Detective Linda allowed herself a moment of weakness and slipped her arm around Kirsten's waist. It was a public display she would not have been comfortable with under most circumstances, but it felt right. Here with her new best friends, in a city she had avoided most of her life for the loss it represented, being emotionally and physically supported by the woman she truly hoped would be the love of her life. Kirsten hadn't waited to be asked to come once she knew what had happened. She'd called Linda from her car as she sped to New York City, assuring her she would be there in record time.

Kyle looked around again while Danny chatted with the women. It seemed so incongruous, that everything could end this way, feeling this good. He felt a moment of guilt for enjoying the night, when it had been preceded by danger and death. Survivor's guilt, he supposed, something he knew well from losing so many friends to AIDS when he was himself a young man. He knew it was just part of living, that the lucky ones made it through the years and had to let go of those who did not.

"We made it," Kyle said, talking to himself.

"What?" Danny asked.

Kyle turned to them, realizing he'd spoken his thought out loud. "Nothing," he said. "Where were we?"

"You and Danny, a weekend in New Hope," Linda said. "The Fourth of July sounds about perfect."

"We can watch the fireworks," Kyle said.

Danny caught his eye, nodding slightly toward Linda and Kirsten. "That we can," he said, smiling. "That we can."

Kyle sipped his wine again, glancing around the gallery. Everyone was there. Everything was in place. Everything was as perfect as it could be.

They had made it.

Death in the Headlights
A Kyle Callahan Mystery

Featuring Detective Linda

Chapter One

Autumn in the Delaware River Valley is spectacular. From the winding Delaware River that can swell with rains to spill wildly over its banks, to the miles upon miles of lush green trees lining the highways and back roads, the area is unquestionably among the most scenic and serene on the East Coast. The change of seasons is dramatic, leaving no doubt what time of year it is: dark green summers with leaves in full fan, springs that give meaning to the experience of renewal, winters bleak and often harsh, and now, October, with the landscape draped in swaths of color, red, yellow, orange, all vying for supremacy in the fall season's palette.

Linda Sikorsky never imagined herself living in the woods. She'd known for many years that most people's ideas of New Jersey were based on late-night comedians' jokes and uninformed ridicule that assumed New Jersey's declining cities were the entire state. But it was called "The Garden State" for a reason: go just a short drive from Newark airport and not far from New York City itself, and you'll find gorgeous riverbanks, forests, farms and small town life. Linda had been accustomed to living in the Valley, having served on the New Hope, Pennsylvania, police force for twenty years, but she had not expected to find herself settling into a house not much bigger than a cottage on the Jersey side, surrounded by ten acres of woods. Her aunt Celeste, sister to her late father Pete, had left her the house in her will. Linda had been to the house many times to visit. She knew Celeste did not get along with her son, Jack, but she never expected to be left the house, in the woods, in such gorgeous, lonesome countryside.

The timing had been impeccable, despite relying on Celeste's sudden death from cardiac arrest as she watered the flower beds on her back porch. Detective Linda Sikorsky was about to retire, leaving the force to open a vintage (she did not care for the term "second hand") store in New Hope.

She'd met her fiancée Kirsten McClellan back in January, and quite suddenly she found herself with a house. It was only twenty minutes from New Hope, and she loved being in the woods. She loved the mile drive up from Highway 29, along a road that wound through trees she called the emerald forest when they were in full leaf. In short, there was no reason for her not to live here, so she'd packed up her apartment and moved in early September, two weeks before retiring. Kirsten remained in her New Hope condo – they weren't ready yet to live together – and Linda happily spent her nights in the woods, while her days were all about preparation: preparing to open her store, *For Pete's Sake*, named after her cop father. Preparing to marry Kirsten, eventually. And now, immediately at hand, preparing for her first overnight visitors, Kyle Callahan and his partner Danny Durban, in from Manhattan to enjoy a weekend in the woods.

***

The four of them were driving home from dinner in Stockton. They'd had one of the best meals Kyle could remember ever having, enjoyed by fireside in the Old Miller Inn. He and Danny had driven by the place a few times on their trips to New Hope, as they explored the surrounding area, but they'd never eaten there. The meal had been exquisite, as had the company. Kyle and Danny had taken quickly to Kirsten, once she'd shown up at Kyle's photography exhibit at the Katherine Pride Gallery that past April. Her devotion to Linda was obvious, and the four of them had been talking about a weekend together ever since.

Tonight they were driving along Route 651, up toward Lockatong Road where Linda now lived. Kyle and Danny had arrived that morning, a leisurely Saturday drive from New York City that included breakfast and some shopping at the Flemington outlets. The day had been perfect, followed by a night of food, friendship and memories. The only thing left now was to visit a short while longer at the house and settle into the guest room for a cozy sleep beneath a thick down comforter.

Linda was driving, chatting with Kirsten in the front seat. Kyle and Danny were in the back, holding hands as they both looked out their side windows at the trees lighted only by the car's headlights. Kyle was about to ask Linda, whom he continued to call Detective Linda despite her retirement, what she and Kirsten would like for the breakfast he was planning to make in the morning, when the car suddenly slammed to a halt, jerking Kyle and Danny forward. Both were wearing seatbelts, and Kyle felt the belt dig into his shoulder.

"What happened?" Kyle said, worried they had hit a deer. The animals were everywhere out here, and they often bounded out in front of cars. A collision could be fatal, and not just for the deer, but there'd been no collision. No thud, no impact.

"There," Linda said, pointing at the side of the road. The car was stopped, and they all followed her line of sight to the left shoulder. Just beyond it, in a pile of leaves that had accumulated in the day's wind, was a woman, next to a bicycle, unmoving.

Linda quickly unfastened her seatbelt and jumped out of the car, followed instantly by the others. A moment later all four of them were standing around a body – for it was a body at this point, clearly deceased – wondering what happened, how, and when. The woman was not dressed for this weather, as if she'd fled on her bicycle at a moment's notice ... or a moment's opportunity to escape. The bike was what Kyle called a "Wicked Witch of the West" bike, large, with those unwieldy handlebars and a basket between them big enough for a small dog. The bicycle was blue, with metallic flecks that shone in the flashlight Linda was using to scan the scene. She knew the woman was dead, but checked for a pulse anyway.

"Call 911," she said, kneeling down and examining the body.

"Already on it," Danny said, his cell phone to his ear as he reached a dispatcher and began explaining what they'd found and where they were.

The dead woman was not young; she looked to be in her sixties, wearing a denim dress and light gray sweater. Her feet were covered only in house slippers, one of which had come off in the collision. And it was clearly a collision. Someone had run this woman over and kept going. Was it a hit-and-run, or deliberate? Why would she be out here like this at night? Did no one else come along this road and see her broken body and her mangled bicycle? And what – or who – had she been running from?

Find out in 'Death in the Headlights: A Kyle Callahan Mystery Featuring Detective Linda', coming spring 2014.

ABOUT THE AUTHOR

I'll break habit here and write in the first person, since you can read my 'Mark McNease has been writing since childhood' bio in several other places. But it's true: I first put pen to paper telling stories about a large stuffed toy dog I had coming to life. I could not have been more than eight years old.

Writing is the one thing I have done consistently all my life, whether it was being expressed in short fiction, long fiction, poetry, prose, plays, or children's television scripts. It is the one thing I have always felt compelled to do. After winning an Emmy in 2001 for Outstanding Children's Program in the Chicago/Milwaukee market, I realized I had been chasing validation for many years, and that now I had it I could let that go and return to writing fiction for love and occasional profit. And here we are.

'Pride and Perilous' is the second book in the Pride Trilogy, to be completed with 'Death by Pride' (a serial killer strikes every Pride weekend in New York City and must be stopped before the East River flows with blood once again). Having discovered what a good team Kyle and Detective Linda make, the muse insisted I take a detour and write a Kyle Callahan Mystery Featuring Detective Linda, which is up next. I see these two couples having several adventures over the next few years, with murder and mayhem along the way.

Thanks to anyone and everyone who has set a spell with Kyle and the gang. I hope you'll take another ride on the mystery train, meet a new traveler or two, and keep me getting up before the sun to bring you more!

As for my personal life, I live in New York City with my partner Frank and our dwindling family of cats. We have a house in the rural New Jersey countryside where we plan to move permanently someday.

Made in the USA
Charleston, SC
12 September 2014